Praise for Benchere In Wonderland

"Plaudits are due for Steven Gillis's brilliant fifth novel, an ambitious treatise on the role of art and the artist in modern day society. Gillis has an uncanny knack for depicting the best and worst of humankind… (while) carefully examining the fallibility and resolve of the artist."

—*Publishers Weekly*

Praise for The Consequence of Skating

"A compelling meditation on media influence and social isolation. Gillis's fourth novel explores the struggle for redemption and acceptance in a world saturated by information."

—*Booklist* ☆☆☆☆☆

Praise for The Law of Strings

"This story collection hooked me from story one and continued to captivate to the end. Expert dialogue and movement and resolution in each piece. This is a book you could read in one sitting…the pace is that swift, the stories that good."

—**Stephen Dixon**, two-time National Book Award finalist

Praise for Temporary People

"Here is a fable for our time, and for just about any other time you can imagine."

—**Chris Bachelder**, finalist for 2016 National Book Award

Praise for Giraffes

"Gillis's stories are illuminatingly strange, filled with power, electric, and will stay with you long after you think you've gone to sleep."

—**Stephen Elliott**, author of *The Adderall Diaries*

Praise for The Weight of Nothing

"Beguilingly mystical!"

—*Publishers Weekly*

Praise for Walter Falls

"An exceptionally well-written novel. *Walter Falls* is highly recommended as a powerful and moving saga of the human condition."

—*Midwest Book Review*

LIARS

A Genuine Vireo Book
an imprint of Rare Bird Books
Los Angeles, Calif.

LIARS

STEVEN GILLIS

THIS IS A GENUINE RARE BIRD BOOK

Rare Bird Books
453 South Spring Street, Suite 302
Los Angeles, CA 90013
rarebirdbooks.com

Set in Minion Pro
Printed in the United States

10 9 8 7 6 5 4 3 2 1

Publisher's Cataloging-in-Publication data
Names: Gillis, Steven, 1957–, author.
Title: Liars / Steven Gillis.
Description: First Paperback Edition | A Genuine Vireo Book | New York, NY;
Los Angeles, CA: Rare Bird Books, 2017.
Identifiers: ISBN 9781644281192
Subjects: LCSH Marriage—Fiction. | Family—Fiction. | Divorce—Fiction.
| Adultery—Fiction. | Authors—Fiction. | Psychological fiction. | BISAC
FICTION / Literary | FICTION / General
Classification: LCC PS3607.I446 L5 2017 | DDC 813.6—dc23

For Mary. Truth. Always.

I wish that people who are conventionally supposed to love each other would say to each other, when they fight, "Please—a little less love, and a little more common decency."

—*Slapstick,* **Kurt Vonnegut**

The truth is always an insult or a joke, lies are generally tastier. We love them. The nature of lies is to please. Truth has no concern for anyone's comfort.

—*Geek Love,* **Katherine Dunn**

She lies and says she's in love with him, can't find / a better man / She dreams in color, she dreams in red, can't find / a better man.

—**"Better Man," Pearl Jam**

CHAPTER ONE

TODAY AT THE MARKET, I saw them for the first time. He was wearing a poplin short-sleeved shirt, untucked, blue and green, beige cargo shorts, and dark weathered sandals. His glasses were Oakley, wire rim, his hair unbrushed, brown, and curling in the summer heat. She was similarly dressed in a gray T-shirt, blue shorts, her hair left loose, her frame shapely with a few extra pounds acquired at the start of middle age. Her purse was a knitted satchel, yellow and green, strung crossways on a strap from her right shoulder to her left hip dividing her breasts.

Together they were pushing one of the smaller carts. Examined separately they were easily ignored, while as a couple, smiling so, chattering and whispering, their fingers and hips with a frequent touch, I couldn't look away. How happy they seemed, smug in their public persona, wanting everyone to believe their relationship was blessed, arranged by Aphrodite, aided by Cupid's arrow, or some such silly thing. Since my divorce I have puzzled over romance, its verisimilitude and relentless ache, and I have come to regard every relationship as its own intimate deception. To me, love is organic, conceived in the heart by way of a chemical reaction, a synaptic impulse with pheromones and dopamine made to dance, the course of any couple's commitment is time-sensitive and marches inevitably toward its own demise. Love grapples as all things do against its physical limitations, its shelf life as it were, the wearing down from age, from compound failure, from boredom and natural change. Over any prolonged period love is unsustainable, of this I am sure; devotion is a fantasy given status through poetry and film, while in the real world such application is as fictional as the Loch Ness Monster, as wanting as Don Quixote's quest.

This is no cynical view forged after Lidia left me. I am no pouting Thomas. I am romantic enough in my own way and have experienced over the years every sort of relationship, brief and extended, sexual and virginal, wistful and wanton. That I failed in my marriage was a consequence of application not effort, or so it seems to me. During our time together, in my effort to address the complexity of keeping a wife, I adhered to a firm belief in the application of free love, convinced the only way to mount a successful relationship was to give it wings. Lidia, too, for a time, believed as much. When we met, I had recently published my first novel, *Kilwater Speaks*. To date, some twelve years later, *Kilwater* remains my only real success. The novel was received well with a handful of reviews yet sold poorly upon release; a parody of our times, a product of youthful ambition up against a thousand other titles, *Kilwater* flatlined out the gate and disappeared.

I had sent a copy of *Kilwater* to a friend who was then an assistant set designer on *The Sopranos*. By chance, one day, he pulled my book from his pocket while at work and placed it in a scene. Delivering his lines, James Gandolfini happened to pick *Kilwater* up off the table, the title flashing out to millions of viewers. By the end of the night, social media had exploded with wonder about the book. New reviews were written revisiting the novel, which achieved instant validation and full ringing support from a new wave of readers leading to accolades and ridiculously high sales.

Based on the success of *Kilwater*, I was offered a chance to teach. The same schools that had turned my applications down before came calling now. I accepted an offer from the university in my hometown. That summer, I attended BookExpo America (BEA) where I partied hard and stumbled through a handful of panel discussions. At some point, I was introduced to Lidia who was finishing her MBA at Bowling Green and doing research for her thesis, which examined the marketing efficiency at carnival-like conferences such as BEA. We bumped into one another a few more times throughout the three days. Lazy in my conceit, I assumed my name and glow from *Kilwater* were all I needed to get her attention. Lidia expected more.

We wound up at the same party on the next to last night of the conference, a gathering in a reserved room at the Langham Hotel. Lidia came with Monica McFawn Robinson, a friend of hers from Bowling Green. I was chatting indiscriminately, looking to get laid, when, in a group to the right of me, P. J. O'Rourke made a disparaging remark about Wesley Clark—he was actually quoting Rush Limbaugh referring to Clark as a "sock puppet"—and Lidia at once turned and dressed O'Rourke down. I was not so much a political person, then or now; rather I was more of a social commentator, an observer of the winds and such, though I did have strong liberal leanings and tended to immerse myself in periods of interest only to lose focus and commitment when my curiosity drew me to something else.

To his credit, O'Rourke was charming as Lidia suggested he'd do better to concentrate on the crimes of the current administration rather than to glibly besmirch an actual American hero like Clark. I needn't have, as Lidia had O'Rourke on the ropes, but I interjected just the same, noting Clark's work with the Open Society Institute and his efforts to improve education, freedom of the press, and public health around the world—this I had only by chance just read. I remember how Lidia had looked at me then, first in her effort to place me, and then disparagingly, as if my effort to chime in was more sexist than chivalrous, more ego-induced and intrusive than helpful at all. "The Open Society Foundation," she corrected me, letting me know the organization had changed its name a few years ago, and as the others dispersed and O'Rourke slipped off, she asked me to tell her what else I knew about the OSF.

I knew nothing, of course, and knew even less about Clark, though I bluffed my way through for a minute or so, until Lidia stopped me again and, with a reference I didn't expect, said, "I thought so. This is the same trouble I had with *Kilwater.*"

I didn't understand, didn't know she had read my book, and was startled by her critique, equally so when she said, "Oh, it's brilliant, yes. Everyone thinks so and you know that. But your observations in *Kilwater* are set on the surface, like makeup, or no, like a juggler who receives our applause for keeping ten balls in the air, but everyone knows eventually the juggling has to stop. You pulled off the novel no doubt, but when I finished I wasn't sure if your most cleverly worded insights were anything more than that and wondered how much you actually understood about the lives you created."

The comment stung not only because I didn't care to hear it, but because I had often thought the same and worried that my writing was just that: a house of cards I could construct with a certain flair but was untenable nonetheless. I stuttered out some comment in turn, some foolish reference to a manuscript being no different than a painting where the text is meant to be representational and not dependent on what the author actually knows, but this, too, came out poorly, and Lidia stopped me, touched my arm, smiled, and said, "It's okay," before turning and walking away.

The next day, at the end of the BEA, Lidia asked me to take her to the airport. I was surprised as I did not think she liked me. We were staying at different hotels and had flights to separate cities, but I agreed and picked her up in my cab. During the drive she asked me to tell her something about myself without mentioning my writing. I thought for a minute then said, "When I'm away from home I miss my dog."

It was enough, I suppose, or maybe she had already made up her mind. Living as we did a few hours' drive apart, we began a relationship with phone calls and weekend visits. I was struggling then to start my second book—for which I had already signed a contract and received an advance—worried about my talent, how to meet expectations, and what exactly I had to say. Falling in love offered me a diversion, and I was falling, as best I knew how, which was mostly from what I read in books.

Six months after we met, Lidia left Ohio and moved in with me. The unexpected payout from *Kilwater* and advance on my second novel enabled me to buy a house with extra bedrooms and a yard for Rex, my dog at the time. Lidia brought her vanity, a gift from her mother, her clothes and books, and a loveseat the color of verbena. She took a job waiting tables at Sere's, a position I didn't quite understand, but she told me not to worry, that she had a plan. In six months she would be managing the restaurant, she said, and in six months she was.

We married the following spring. A year later Lidia purchased a space on Verne and Fourth, using money drawn from two silent investors and nothing from me. That spring she opened Caber Hills, a slightly upscale restaurant and bar. In no time Caber Hills became a success. Lidia paid off her investors, expanded the building, and created a local organic menu of meats and vegetables, fish and cheese, which she changed and added seasonally to the menu. Her industry was a marvel to me and inspired me to hunker down and address the challenge of my second book.

However motivated, the effort took time; my attempt then was to write a book about a man who fell in love with his doppelganger's wife. I struggled to clarify my ideas, threw out hundreds of pages, started over, veered around, and doubled back. After five years, I finally finished and watched as the success of *Kilwater* shined a light on my new novel. There were articles written, interviews and reviews, and all sorts of discussion as to whether I caught lightning in a bottle twice. The short answer was I did not. Where *Kilwater* was a timely blend of youthful angst, observation, and humor, *A Full Fog Front* veered toward a more mature narrative for which I wasn't entirely ready. At best my sophomore effort was called ambitious, my saber touch intact, though most reviews were indifferent with some going so far as to say the book was a misstep.

"Not to worry," Lidia said. A long career, she told me. You hit the notes you wanted and next time, she was sure. Oh, she was giddy with the success of her restaurant, and my poor little book she was hardly concerned about. Baffled, I took my new novel out on tour. The stores and audiences were happy to have me, though they mostly wanted to talk about *Kilwater*. I missed Lidia, though somehow it was also a relief to be away. Up until then our marriage had proceeded mostly without issue. Lidia was busy and so was I. We were happy together, didn't quarrel much, didn't doubt our relationship in any tangible way, and were consensual in our satisfaction, and while we did discuss having kids this somehow didn't happen and we tried not to dwell.

Sexually, we were quite compatible; we had similar tastes and preferences, were open-minded in our views, fearless to the extent we allowed ourselves to be. We shared our fantasies and desires with one another, which we then played out as games designed for two. As Caber Hills grew in success, life became more defined for us, the mystery of who we were individually and collectively made clearer, our ability to point at one another and say, *Ahh yes, that's who you are.*

The question then became whether we were satisfied with our answers or wanted more. The wondering, on my part, was not so much an issue of displeasure as it was doubt, a feeling that I couldn't possibly sustain whatever it was that made Lidia love me, the mystery of it all, and that such a thing as love was too powerful a force to be contained in any sort of tight-grip fashion, and that we could not continue on together to the exclusion of all supplementary emotional interests without eventually growing resentful of each other. In an effort to address this dilemma, I decided to test myself. It was a big step. In five years I had not been with anyone but Lidia, though there were temptations and flirtations, a few extracurricular toes-in-the-water amounting to nothing. I knew I loved Lidia, though what if there was more to love than sustaining social norms, constrictive monogamy, and marital decorum? What if real love required a different kind of trust and liberation?

Two days later, I flew west and read at Powell's. A reception was arranged for me afterward and I struck up a conversation with a woman in a maroon top, gray jeans, and black ankle-high boots. Over cocktails she questioned me about A Full Fog Front, accused me of writing a bromance and deliberately leaving women at the periphery of my book. "So tell me," she asked, "are you a misogynist or are you gay?"

Her comment was intentionally baiting. I took the bait, took her for more drinks after the reception, took her back to my hotel room where she took off my clothes and danced with me to music by Prince playing on the clock radio. Mounted and mounting, kissed and kissing, probed and probing, I explored my reaction while sexing my Portland playdate. She was moderately attractive, eagerly limber like a bodacious stick of licorice, her nipples tasting of almonds, her pubes shaved down to a cherubic peach. Over hills and into valleys, I felt no guilt to speak of, no worry or alarm. Despite what seemed an extemporaneous tryst, I continued to think about the properties of my marriage and to what extent my feelings for Lidia remained unbowed. Waiting for my answer, as we finished, I went so far as to talk about my marriage, compared and contrasted, and announced without apology, "This was fun and I still love my wife."

At home, I waited to see if I would crumble in Lidia's presence. When this didn't happen, I tested myself again. And again. It was intriguing at first, and then I began to mull the consequences of my manifest, whether my intention was to be a secret philanderer forever or if my inspiration was legitimate, and I honestly believed the best manner of marriage was liberal and free. If I did truly believe the latter, what sort of selfish display was I conducting if I refused to share as much with my wife?

I considered the prospect, weighed the risk, and ultimately decided to open my theory up to discussion. Casually at first the idea was presented. We spoke of how individualism is the greatest gift we can allow the people we love, the freedom to explore and express ourselves, the courage to know that true love supports an open-minded approach to relationships and that we need to be embracing of all that fulfills us and not be forced by tradition to maneuver and manage our relationship toward some safe middle ground. Such narrow values, I argued, were about control and had little to do with love.

Our talks were just that for a time, though Lidia soon began broaching the subject on her own. She was no less liberal and inviting of nontraditional views, and was intrigued by the idea of exploring love outside the proverbial box. That winter we arranged a getaway and drove north. Lidia wanted to take me skiing. I am not a skier, I prefer the comfort of the fireplace and a large warm toddy, and watching ski bunnies pass by the window with the frosted glint of snow outside. I bundled myself just the same and went with Lidia on rented skies up the hill where we took a lesson.

The instructor assigned to us was a handsome man in a blue parka vest and the thinnest of leggings despite the cold. He wore a knitted cap pushed back off his ears, high on his head, his chiseled cheeks, as I recall, freshly shaven. We were a small group and Lidia took a liking to our instructor right away. I studied the scene, assessed any encroaching sense of jealousy weighed against potential promise, and found I was okay. On the hillside, in that moment, in the dead of winter, I was excited, and as our instruction ended and Lidia prepared to ski, she made sure to get our teacher's attention.

Fresh snow had fallen, and over the soft powder Lidia and our teacher sped down the hill while I duck-stepped sideways and slid over the smallest of safe distances. Lidia was a much more advanced skier, so I spent the day watching my wife wave as she passed me coming and going. Later, she went to a larger hill and I didn't see her for some time. Back at the lodge, she appeared in our room rosy cheeked and exhilarated from her day and eager to make love. I was accommodating, though in the middle insisted she tell me what she was thinking. Hesitant at first, she finally confided and our sex became feral.

We parted again the next day as I remained on the smallest slope while Lidia went hunting for further adventure. I retreated to the lodge early, went upstairs, worked for a bit, came back down, and sat by the window with a drink where I soon saw them together. At dinner that night we spoke and it was then I suggested we not be cavalier about our experiences and that she should treat herself to the fullest extent of what she deserves. "This has everything to do with our love," I said and insisted I was not threatened and understood her desires absolutely.

She excused herself before dessert, went upstairs, fixed her face, and then departed. I did not see her again until after midnight. We slept closely and skied once more the following day before leaving the mountain. A gray covering had rolled in overnight and the snow that came with it was thick and put ice on our skis and the tracks we covered. I felt bold and tried my hand on a higher hill before we left. The whole trip down, gathering speed without control, I heard the wind through the trees and the creak of frozen branches.

CHAPTER TWO

OUR MARKET IS LIKE most of the others in the city: nouveau-centric, organic, catering to young professionals and folks suddenly conscious about their health. Curious then, for reasons still visceral and not well-thought-out, I followed the couple through the aisles as they stopped for milk and coffee, for bread and wine, for fish and vegetables and meat. Twice she placed her hand on his back. He leaned toward her and whispered something and she laughed. They seemed quite happy, and more than that, haughty in their contentedness, which annoyed me as if their display were meant as a personal attack.

Determined, I gave chase. At the meat counter I also purchased ground beef and fish. For a moment, I thought I'd lost track of the couple, then found them again near the chips. The woman had her fingers still on the man's back, the man with his head tipped toward her. When they reached the checkout line, the man squeezed the woman's hand. She got into a conversation with the cashier about this being the best season for in-state strawberries. "The best," she said, and her voice was filled with delight.

He slid down to the end of the counter and bagged their groceries. She was still talking as he took out his wallet and paid. His wallet was brown and slightly worn. The cashier asked to see his ID for the wine, a standard market policy now despite their age. His wife couldn't resist making a joke and at this, too, he laughed.

~

GLORIA IS IN THE front room watching TV when I get home. It's after six and she has on the news. *MSNBC Live.* I put the groceries down on the kitchen counter and pour myself a drink. Gloria comes into the kitchen and unwraps her fish. Shortly after my divorce from Lidia, Gloria came to Colossal, the recording studio I own, and introduced herself to me. How I came to own a recording studio is one of those odd incidents that happens in life when all of one's attention is elsewhere.

I was a few years into my marriage, drinking more than I should, struggling to get my second novel started, when a friend brought me to the Bili Club. A singer-songwriter duo called Group Witness was performing that night. The pair played original tunes; they reminded me of Damien Rice and Dallas Green, though without the depth and intuitive command of their songs. After the show, my friend took me backstage where I told the musicians exactly what I thought of their performance.

My critique was listened to politely. As I was Eric McCanus, author of *Kilwater Speaks*, I was indulged and not run from the room. I spoke with a drunkard's arrogance, claiming to hear in their songs the music that was missing. Although my knowledge of music was limited, my abilities on piano less than marginal then, I knew what I liked and understood the creative process without having to sing or read a note. To their credit, Group Witness gave me a CD of their songs and an invitation to the rehearsal they were having the next day.

I went home and reviewed their work in progress, and I could hear again the direction I thought their sound should take. I made notes for adding arrangements with keyboard, saxophone, and drums, adjusted their guitars away from a folky strum to more of a pick and echo; all of this evolving from the hum whistle beat in my head. I also changed the chorus on three of their tunes, changed the opening line in their best song, then came and presented my ideas at their rehearsal.

Already under contract with Front Row Records, Group Witness tested my suggestions at their rehearsal and then again with a full band. A recording was made. Front Row dug the sound. The song "Carried to Shore" was rerecorded, picked up by independent stations, gained momentum, looped into airplay on the bigger broadcasts in over two hundred cities, became a solid hit, and launched Group Witness on a national tour. From this, Front Row called to see if I was interested in working with any more of their upcoming talent.

The way things happen, right? The first four groups assigned to me wound up with songs on the radio while strong sales put cash in my pocket. Other musicians and record companies began calling; with my reputation in the industry expanding, I decided to formalize my good fortune and bought Colossal. I hired the best people to help me record and manage artists of our own. Ten years later I have a nice gig going, have worked with great artists, and have made serious money; all this while my own career as a writer has circled the drain like a gummy brown turd in a rest stop stall.

~'

GLORIA WEARS CANVAS SHOES with no arch. Although she is thin, her feet are large and the shoes narrow, causing the weight of her foundation to spill out. I used to like her feet; I would celebrate them along with other features that were new to me once but less so now. The first time Gloria came to Colossal, I was working with a band called Nickity Split. Gloria arrived uninvited and asked to play for me. This sort of impromptu request happened often. Most days I was polite and told folks they could leave a demo, email me a link, or make an appointment to come by and for twenty bucks I would listen. It wasn't about the money, but if someone really wanted to be heard they'd come up with the cash. I gave Gloria the standard reply, then went about my business.

Dressed in jeans and a T-shirt, her hair cut short, her guitar in a black case with stickers from Modesto and South by Southwest, she appeared to be like most musicians I knew. No one noticed her sitting down and taking out her guitar, but soon the studio was filled with her music. Her voice was rich, a sort of Jonatha Brooke meets Rickie

Lee Jones—a fullness in the sound she knew how to control. Her guitar was an old Martin, her song of choice an original with a hook phrase line, *You can't tell me to go / when you already know / I'm gone.* I turned around and listened. When she finished, I walked over and said, "That's going to cost you twenty bucks."

I couldn't be sure if she knew I was joking but deadpan she replied, "How about I just blow you and we call it even?" Who couldn't laugh at that? I invited her to stick around and had her sing backup on a tune we were recording. We went to dinner that night and went back to my place where I told her about Lidia and how I was still coming to terms with our divorce.

Gloria kissed me and said, "Listen to you." She drove an old Ford Focus and had a blue duffel bag she didn't bring inside until the third night. Fred, my dog after Rex, took to Gloria. Fred did not like all the women I introduced him to. Gloria liked Fred but didn't fawn over him to impress me. When we had sex, I shut Fred in the hall. Gloria told me she was from Kansas, was thirty, and had come east on a caravan tour of small clubs with two other acts. There was a fallout, a best-laid-plans scenario, which left her here looking for work. She slept for a time on the couch of a woman she had met at the Pickle Pub and was renting a room now month to month over on Kettering Street. Three days a week she served the late-breakfast-to-lunch crowd at Danny Karats, a popular downtown diner. She played local gigs, solo mostly, had some contacts and session work, and was, as everyone else, looking for more.

I sort the groceries on the counter, get out a pan for my burger, and grab a pan for Gloria's fish, which will take longer to prepare. If I were generous, if I were kind, I would delay the cooking of my burger, would occupy myself in some other way—refilling my drink, setting the table, talking to Gloria while timing things so that our foods finished together. Instead I'm not like this tonight, am distracted and thinking still of what I saw at the market.

Gloria butters her pan, seasons her fish, and puts it in the oven. I flip my burger and look for cheese. When my food is done, I serve myself, take my drink and plate to the table. Gloria checks her fish, finds the receipt from the market, looks to see how much the meal will cost her.

~

TOMORROW I WILL WRITE:

In their kitchen, he turned the oven on for her fish while she found a pan for his burger and made him a patty. He set the table, fixed himself a drink, asked if she would like a glass of wine. Their kids come and go, home briefly for the summer, old enough to have lives of their own. They talked together through their meal, their tone with one another familiar and light. After dinner they sat outside with their drinks. He pulled the ottoman in front of her chair and volunteered to massage her feet. She had large feet, thick butternut toes he spread with his fingers, applying the calendula ointment she liked. In their younger days, her legs were nicely curved cinnamon stalks, sinewy and smooth. Age had added to the skin and muscle. He placed his hands palms up so her heel could rest inside, took the beat down spread of her arch, and rubbed with his thumbs, through the skin and deeper.

~

AFTER DINNER GLORIA KISSES me and heads out. I don't ask where she's going and she doesn't tell me. Sometimes she tells me, though rarely do I ask. If she has a gig, I go sometimes and listen, and sometimes I don't. When I go off without her, I sometimes say where I am going even if where I'm going is nowhere Gloria needs to know about. Although we have been living together now for over eight months, I have never told Gloria that I love her. I believe I still love Lidia, though this is unlikely and more an excuse, I think, to not love Gloria. Since coming to stay with me, since living with me and sleeping together most nights, Gloria has not once said she loves me. We have not discussed our relationship, allowing one another to come and go as we will and as we want, as I want and Gloria, too; and through all this we manage to function with an openness Lidia and I aimed for but never really managed to pull off.

I tell myself Gloria must be going to meet friends, though I suspect she has a date. She has changed her clothes and brushed her hair. Our arrangement does not preclude Gloria from seeing other men. She has gone out before and on occasion not come home. I am fine with this. Other than what risk this poses, STDs and such, I have no concerns and would not complain if Gloria came to me one day and said she had fallen in love. I believe this and also believe she wishes me the same, though we do not talk of it ever.

Gloria advocates open relationships, and still she is critical when I tell her about Lidia and me; she is not surprised things went south, says a couple can't party-fuck their way through a marriage. "You have to actually believe in what you're doing."

"We did believe," I argued and told her again how I thought if Lidia and I were more open in this way our relationship would evolve into something enlightened.

"Why?"

"Why did I think that?"

"No, why would you want that? Who says enlightenment is anything great?" We were in bed when this conversation happened. I remember Gloria naked on the sheet and me sitting up, naked as well and trying to decide if she was serious. I asked how could enlightenment be anything but remarkable, which caused her to look at me as if I was truly naïve and answer, "Enlightenment doesn't exist, McCanus. Not in any obtainable way. You're talking about a higher level of awareness, which, for most people, is the difference between distinguishing lime and jade. It doesn't matter. We're simple creatures really, with simple needs. How many people do you think can actually handle being enlightened?"

It was a curious question and not one I was sure I could answer though I said just the same, "Enlightenment may be hard to obtain but it's still worth pursuing."

"Is it? Don't you think most people have more immediate concerns? Being better to ourselves and others, getting through the day without harm, isn't that enough without having to worry about being enlightened? This life, McCanus, isn't complicated unless you make it so. The most important thing we can do in life," Gloria said, "is learn how to be happy. Whatever sense of enlightenment we achieve comes from this. If we can be happy without hurting anyone else along the way that's enlightenment. All the rest is garbage." She went to the window then, still naked, and smoked.

~

LATER, I AM WITH my lover. My lover is not Gloria. My lover is not Lidia now. My lover is my lover. Driving to see my lover, I think back to what Gloria said before about happiness and consider how I had never thought of happiness in terms of enlightenment, had always somehow believed enlightenment was on a higher plane and not that being happy was a minor achievement, but who after all was ever truly happy? The couple at the market? I seriously doubted. I recalled then the Tolstoy quote in *Anna Karenina*, how all happy families were said to be happy in the same way while unhappy families were unique in their misery. I disagreed with this, convinced all misery came from the same place, from the failed attempt to love and be loved. Despite what Tolstoy wrote, there was nothing unique about Anna Karenina's despair. Her mistake was all too common, her belief in love was what ruined her; her refusal to understand that relationships were fragile and ephemeral mostly, untenable over time. Failing to recognize the futility of love and happiness was a fool's trap for sure and is what caused poor Anna to take a leap grounded in anything but faith.

My lover likes to fuck until we are completely exhausted. A nearly insatiable bird, afterward we collapse, warm on the blanket, warm in the sheets, warm in the warm spoon cradle I lie, as does she. Prone, yes, I am prone here, prone in every way, turning flatback to her though she wants to cling. If she had been the first to roll away, I would have reached for her. But I manage to be the first to move and with that she tries to find me.

"It's time," I say.

She dresses before I do, lingers halfway with her shorts slipped on as she searches for her shirt. I like the power of being naked in front of her. Somehow being naked as we speak allows me to feel that all my words are true. What possibly can I hide standing before her bare and bared this way as I say, "The weather seems to be changing." In no hurry to dress now, I watch her find all she needs, scattered there across the floor as if a storm had come not too long before and undressed her.

We are wordless otherwise, for the moment at least. Groans and grunts prior, if anything of substance was said I don't recall. I get up and part the blinds. Miles away the horned larks sing. I stand naked in front of the pane and imagine I can hear them.

~

IN THE MORNING I tried to write, but my effort was worse than usual and for this I blamed the couple at the market. My memory of them had become disruptive and was making a mockery of my current narrative, a story I had struggled to tell since *A Full Fog Front* crashed and burned, and how was I supposed to write of love as a danger when I couldn't stop visualizing the two of them floating merrily through the produce aisle like Odysseus and Penelope on MDMA? It occurred to me then, in order to keep writing and to disprove what I thought I witnessed, I had to see them again.

I drove to the market around noon and again on my way home from Colossal. As it was summer, I wasn't teaching, so the university was generous with my schedule—over the last few years I had reduced my course load to one class a semester and nothing from June through August. The university was fine with this, their interest only in keeping my name and *Kilwater* associated with their English department. I went to the market again the following afternoon and that night as well, returned on my way home from Colossal the day after and again the day after that. I went once more that night and then again the next afternoon following a walk with Fred.

Frustrated, I was beginning to wonder if I had possibly made them up, had exaggerated their relationship and was looking for a reason to not finish my book. Uncertain then what I should do, I wandered back toward the exit where at last I saw them. Near the deli section, pushing their cart, her with her fingers on his back while he had his head turned in order to talk, smiling in that way he did when his eyes alighted on her, they were exactly as before, cloying and nauseatingly engaged. Such a disappointment, such a sad sight, how angry it made me, this canard they were perpetuating, this false display no one wished to see. How was anyone to have faith in the universe if such false prophets were allowed to parade themselves freely through our streets and markets? *For the good of everyone, then,* I thought for the first time, *something must be done.*

I followed them through the aisles, looked for signs of anything that might be different. Beyond the slight variation in their clothes, nothing had changed. Hip to hip they walked, merrily so, in stride and in tune, inseparable. Even when placing an item in their cart the task was done in tandem. At the checkout line he held her hand. Incensed, I went out to the parking lot, waited as they returned to their car, and from there I tailed them home.

They lived halfway between the market and my house, on Centre Street, in one of the modest Cape Cod–style homes built in the 1930s. I have always liked the older houses, with their classic architecture, smart lines, and craftsmanship impossible to find today. My house is larger, more modern in design, a contemporary casting with a flat roof and windows everywhere. I texted their address and license plate number to my phone, went home, and ran a computer search. I thought I could discover their names this way, could root around and find additional information, but I was inexperienced and had no luck.

Gloria came home and asked what I was doing. "Nothing," I told her. "Honestly, nothing."

~

FITFUL, I FAILED TO sleep, struggled through my morning's writing, waited just long enough, then drove back to Centre Street that afternoon and got the names of my besotted pair off the mail in their box. Home again, I ran a new series of searches, the process easier now. I soon had information on both. He was Matthew Geere, a high school English teacher, a PhD in theoretical poetics, author of two collections of poetry brought out by a small indie press. I'd never heard of him, had never read him, and how good could he be if he was still teaching high school? I tracked down some of his work, ordered his collections, and read two poems and an essay he wrote on Elizabeth Bishop online.

She was Cara Benz, a landscape architect in charge of the landscaping department at SunGreen Nursery. There were pictures of her from years ago when hale youth and confidence flattered her. I searched for more and found random posts, learned of projects she had designed and constructed, an impressive list including public gardens and private ventures. I read their wedding announcement from twenty years ago, discovered they now had two kids, a boy and a girl, both college age. Matt volunteered at the Outer House for troubled teens. Cara occasionally acted in plays put on by the Blackbird Theater. They seemed to have no religious affiliation, no church or temple, both were on Facebook and Twitter but with limited postings. Once I'd assembled this information, I had no idea what to do with it. Having their names and biographical sketches helped confirm their existence, but did nothing to inform me about their relationship.

I turned off my computer, went downstairs, and poured myself a drink. My cellphone rang and I answered it, heard Lidia say, "Sorry,

sorry. I butt-dialed you," and then she hung up. Perfect, right? I refilled my glass, tried to laugh but couldn't quite. Of all the sad affairs, what more could drive a man to drink?

~

GLORIA HAD A GIG that night, and rather than go with her, I stayed home and outlined a sketch of Cara and Matt's affair. Having completed his graduate degree at the university prior to starting his teaching career at Benniman High School, Matt took a summer job as a mason, mixing mortar, laying bricks with the muscle in his arms. It was a good job and he welcomed the chance to be outdoors. He was excited for the opportunity to teach in the fall, he had not yet seriously considered college jobs, had only published three poems to date, had no track record to speak of, and had no connections other than a few friends teaching at small universities far from home.

He came to the nursery where she was working to pick up supplies and saw her moving through the shop, marking materials for her own projects. Her hair then was a deep reddish-brown pulled back behind her head, her skin tanned, her arms and legs well-toned. The shorts she wore were bibbed overalls cut off above the knee. He watched her, as did all the other summer dirt monkeys, each of them young enough to believe in the beauty of their tribe, their hunger howls and hammer hearts and no shame in their desire. They asked her out, laughed and spoke with her while he hung back; shy in the tangle of aisles and dirt and brick and stone he was sent to gather, he loaded his truck, came around each day, and loaded again.

Cara noticed him, said nothing, waited, found him one day by his truck, his radio playing Richie Havens' "Freedom," from Woodstock, loud as he lifted the weight of his supplies. She came over, clipboard in hand, under the pretext of checking his order. "Richie Havens," she said and stopped to listen. They spoke then and she asked why he never spoke with her before. He said, "You always seemed busy."

He came back after work, stained with sweat and nervous. They went for a drink. The next night, cleaned up, they went to dinner, and went to his apartment where they lay on his bed and spoke of poets and gardens. He did not read her any of his poems, but she found a piece of paper with scrawled lines: *Here beneath / the wet putty stick mortar seal / holding me together / I pile / what comes to my hand / coarse brick upon brick / not for walls but houses.* They ordered a late-night pizza and didn't leave his room until morning. By the time he started teaching at Benniman they were living together on the bottom floor of a house rented on Charleston. They married the following summer. She was three months pregnant and he was enraptured, learning still the ways to make her happy.

~

I DRIVE BY THEIR house again the next day. Matt is there this time, waiting for Cara on the stoop out front. I park a safe distance away and watch as she pulls up. He comes from the steps, goes to greet her, kisses her, and carries her bag inside.

Back home, I take Fred for a walk. The summer heat causes me to sweat. I am jumpy, my novel-in-progress is not in progress at all, it is harder than ever to construct, with each line I write shouting back at me *Liar! Liar! Liar!* now that I have seen them. What am I to do? Despite what I have witnessed, I refuse to believe they are truly happy, I am certain I have accidentally stumbled into some period of reconciliation, some moment of nostalgia or reprieve that all relationships pass through. The story of my new novel is of a cuckold man hounded by love and so fooled by the vanity of his own convictions that he refuses to believe his wife is unfaithful. His devotion, at first an irritant, slowly becomes accepted, and then embraced by the wife who falls back in love with her husband only at the very moment he has abandoned all hope, resentful of his wife's past treatment and determined then to leave her.

Love is at best a fever, a condition ordained by chance and sustained only as long as a white cap wave. Love is as brief as a hiccup, as fragile as a spider's web, as unreliable as a politician's pledge, as valueless as a broken molar. This is what I want to write, have tried to write, and what am I to do now that Matt and Cara have thrown everything into chaos?

Gloria is in the front room as I return, sitting in what has become her favorite chair, the large green cushioned one, which she can fold herself up in and play her guitar. I leave her there and go off to shower. Coming from the bathroom, I walk downstairs naked, and, hoping to divert my thoughts from more serious matters, I say of my ready cock, "Honey, look what I found."

Gloria is playing an original tune on her guitar. She stops and stares at me as I appear, shakes her head, and says, "Looks like you missed a spot."

"What, this?" I wiggle some more.

Unimpressed, Gloria asks, "Do you want to fuck me, Eric?"

"The thought crossed my mind."

"Did it now?" Gloria finds fault with my approach, says that I've been churlish for days, "But now that you're horny and looking for a place to cook your meat."

"Jesus," I say.

"It is a religious experience, I know."

"Apparently, we have a different opinion about what's going on here."

"You don't want to fuck?"

"I do. I didn't think we were going to have a conversation about it first."

"You're an asshole," Gloria goes back to playing her guitar.

I concede, "That may be true."

"A little common decency," Gloria half-sings. "You want to fuck, that's cool. Just be nice to me."

"I am nice."

"You're charitable when you want to be. That doesn't make you nice."

"Okay."

"If we're friends, you need to behave."

"We are friends," I say.

"As friends, then, why don't you tell me what's been going on with you the last few days? You've been weird, McCanus." She shifts and uses the neck of her guitar to point at my dick, which has shrunk back down to a soft cheese.

I start to say it's nothing, that it's just my head being in an odd place, my struggling to write and all the rest, but this is common knowledge and Gloria wants to know, "What else?"

I tell her then about the couple at the market, about Matt and Cara as I haven't mentioned until now, how they appeared to me and seeing them got me thinking.

"About what?"

"About love and happiness."

Gloria strums the tune of "Peace, Love, and Happiness" by G. Love and Special Sauce.

I describe everything in detail, explain how seeing Cara and Matt as they were, as happy together as a Turtles song, rattled me, and that I don't trust couples who flaunt their happiness in public. Gloria asks how I know Cara and Matt are actually in a long-term relationship and I admit then to having followed them home, to rooting through their mail, and researching them online.

"McCanus!" Gloria puts her guitar down. Intrigued now, a mischievous girl, she wags her finger and says, "Seriously, Mac? Why would you do that?"

I'm still standing there naked while Fred the dog lies across the floor, panting from our walk. I answer in terms of my novel and how what I saw at the market tested my perception and screwed up my narrative.

"And so you stalked them?"

"I didn't stalk them."

"You followed them home. You rifled through their mail. You researched them online."

"I was curious."

"Why?"

"I told you."

"You told me what you did. You haven't told me why."

"Didn't I?" I say again it's about my book but Gloria doesn't believe me.

"This isn't about your writing," she says.

"Sure it is. I can't write what I don't believe and I don't believe what I saw."

"But you're not writing about them. You're writing about the opposite of them."

"Exactly."

Gloria shifts in the chair, gives me a look, then asks, "So now what?"

I answer that there is no now, that I'm done with the couple.

"So why follow them?"

"To see."

"What?"

"Who they are."

"But you don't know anything more about who they are now than their names and occupations."

I toss my head back and stare at the ceiling as Gloria asks again, "What are you up to, McCanus?"

I do not answer her question with anything more than what I've already said. I do not say that I stalked Matt and Cara because

I want to expose the deceit of their happiness, that I followed them home because I need to know what they showed me at the market was fragmentary and not representational because it messes with my understanding of the universe to think of them as actually in love and happy. Instead I say, "Hell," insist Gloria needn't be so suspicious and that I'd appreciate her being a bit more sensitive when it's clear I'm struggling.

"Poor baby," Gloria says. "Come here." Her feet are bare. She removes her shirt, peels off her pants, and tells me to lie on the floor. "Let's collaborate," she says.

Afterward, I go back upstairs, get dressed, and return to my writing room, but the prospect of accomplishing anything more creative today is lost. I come down a short while later. Gloria is in the shower now. I think of the things she said and ask myself as she did, *What are you up to, McCanus?* The answer I give is not the answer I know to be true. I go to bed early, get up the next morning and walk with Fred, then try again to write. Distracted, unable to think clearly, I grab my keys and wallet, drive to the nursery, and introduce myself to the woman in charge.

CHAPTER THREE

C ARA JOKES WITH THE college boys who work for her as summer hands. They tease her as she tries to lift heavy bags of peat, this before she shows them the strength of experience and uses her legs and hips to toss the bags onto a hand cart, and moves the load out to her truck. Inside again, she checks her messages; she has just returned from a project on the north end of town and will be heading back out shortly when a man in jeans and a dark T-shirt approaches and asks if they might talk.

~

WE STAND BETWEEN ROLLS of fencing. Cara is a few inches shorter than me, she is dressed for work in bibbed shorts and Wolverine work boots, her arms and face tan, her hair pulled back, her features large, her cheeks high and round, her eyes green and examining. She's hurried but polite and listens as I describe my yard and how I want to have the space redone. I have come up with this idea while driving over, a way to get to know her better. I go ahead and say that I've a large yard, nearly half an acre of open grounds in back. I ask about the prospect of creating a two-tiered space, with Japanese paving stones, flowering trees and plants. It's unclear to me what this will look like or cost. I tell Cara that I am getting preliminary estimates and would like her to enter a bid.

Cara takes me into her office and has me fill out an information sheet. Reviewing the form, it's unclear whether or not she recognizes my name. She doesn't ask if I'm *that* Eric McCanus, explains instead how busy she is and that most of her SunGreen jobs are scheduled weeks in advance. I suggest freelance and that she might consult with me on her own time. She proves scrupulous, says that since I contacted her at SunGreen the project should be maintained as such. I respect her integrity and tell her so. This seems to please her and she promises to stop by my house by the end of the week.

~

I SPEND A FEW hours at Colossal and return home just after four and walk Fred. Gloria is playing solo at The Curve tonight. When she comes home from work I tell her that I plan on going to her gig. She smiles in a way that lets me know tonight is no good. We circle one another in the front room. I decide not to mention my going to see Cara; I hold off on this as I'm sure Gloria will gloat. I head upstairs, take care of some business, deal with university chores, return a few calls, and come down and eat a turkey sandwich from slices of meat I find in the fridge. Later, after Gloria leaves, I remain restless and decide to go to Caber Hills for a drink.

It's almost eight as I reach the restaurant. During our marriage, Lidia worked most evenings and I assume the same is true now. The downstairs dining area has fifteen tables and all are full as I come in. The bar is white and silver, very modern, post-deco with sleek edges and high metal stools. The second floor has an open landing with a private dining room for parties and events. I order two beers at the bar then go upstairs where Lidia keeps her office.

I've been thinking more about Lidia these last few days and this, too, I blame on Matt and Cara. The resolution of our divorce has not entirely quieted the complexity of my feelings, and while our parting remains amicable and we've stayed in touch, I've yet to fully put my affections to rest. In moments of solitude I sometimes harbor a deep wistful sadness, which threatens to turn into regret. Lidia professes none of the same, regards everything that happened as fodder for moving forward. After our skiing trip, we decided to increase our level of experimentation, convinced such enterprise heightened our passion and intimacy toward one another. As partners, we remained open with our encounters, conjoined in the quest, honest and progressive with our participation. Together we constructed a full philosophy behind our sex, a belief that to experience actual freedom the exercise could not be seized at selfishly but had to be offered as a gift from someone else. My offering to Lidia, and Lidia to me, allowed us to be free in ways other couples were not. We tried a few parties, tried a few dates, tried some adlibbed adventures at hotel bars and nightclubs, made one trip to Texas and another to LA. Emancipative, we avoided still any obsession, understood these games were part of a bigger picture, and treated our activities as a hobby—the way other couples took up golf or ballroom dancing all in good fun.

This was during the time my inability to get a third book started was becoming a problem. Fortunately, things at Colossal were going well. I was working with a handful of bands a month, had a fantastic staff managing and recording a larger stable of musicians, and was making good money without having to break a sweat. Producing songs was more of an organic process for me, while composing a novel required a level of concentration I seemed suddenly to lack. Unable to write anything I thought might eventually be good, I became surly and impatient, which caused Lidia to react in kind. Against our agreement, I slept with other women without my wife's consent. Lidia would confront me and I would confess, would try and justify, would say it was just an extension of our views though no, of course, I would not want her to do the same, and yes, I was sorry, and no, there was no emotional involvement, it was just sex, just a way to pass an hour and it was wrong of me, I know, and I appreciate ever so much her understanding.

That she did understand, or was never angry enough to use this as our final straw, was a credit to her. Still we found ourselves adrift, our attention turned inward toward our own work, our own ambitions, and less on our marriage. From this we quarreled incessantly. Where once we were a couple inclined to argue for sport, enjoying the heady back and forth, our words began to sour beneath the point of pleasure and bruise the flesh. Then Lidia had an affair. The affair didn't last.

As arrogant as this sounds, I believe it wasn't meant to. Lidia and I reconciled. I tried to recover, tried to forgive and be forgiven for my own indiscretions, tried to commit, to move forward and keep to the plan we set out. Lidia, too, was well-intended, and still our effort failed with the ineffectiveness of applying tape to a tear in a vein. Rather than heal together, we carved out a place where we conducted ourselves like two wounded cubs sharing a lair, licking our cuts and bruises until we were slathered completely and could lick no more.

~

TONIGHT THERE IS A group inside the private dining area of Caber Hills talking and laughing loudly. Lidia's office is a small space farther back. Her door is locked and I can see through the glass that her light is off. Disappointed, I call her cell and say, "Hey," when she answers.

"Hey, stranger." Lidia is friendly with me, less inclined to be confused by the circumstance of our divorce, and has allowed us to remain close. I ask how she's doing, tell her where I am, that I'm actually at the restaurant now. "Outside your office," I say, "with two beers in hand. I came by for us to have a drink though it seems we missed one another." I ask for news, tell her about my plans for a garden and how I'm looking to reconfigure the yard, which I hope she will like. Lidia says she's sure she will like it fine, then adds that her opinion doesn't matter as the garden belongs to me now, the house too, the deal we made when we divorced as Lidia wanted to move downtown.

"All the same," I do not tell her about Cara and Matt, say instead that I imagined the new landscape with her in mind.

Lidia doesn't bite; she asks about Gloria instead. I say she's good and ask about the sous chef she's seeing, and Lidia says, "He's a sous chef," and we laugh at this. I do not talk more about Gloria, do not mention anything about my writing or why again it has stalled, I am feeling something else, a need to tell Lidia that I still love her. Whether or not I do still love her is something else again, is a new thing to blame on Matt and Cara, and hedging I say, "I miss you."

"You missed me already," Lidia in reply.

"Either way, I think we should get back together."

"All right. I'll be right over."

"I'm serious," I tell her.

"No you're not. And no you don't."

I already regret saying this much, modify my claim and confess to feeling nostalgic, to missing our late nights hanging out at Caber Hills. Lidia responds with a sing-song repeat of my name. "Eric, Eric, Eric." Since leaving me, since our divorce, we haven't slept together, we have done nothing more than talk, though when I get to chattering on this way Lidia knows, the insinuation clear, she says that I should let the moment pass.

"I don't understand."

"Yes, you do."

I do, it's true. I stop then, and when Lidia admits it's nice that I came by but we should leave things as they are I decide not to press, have learned at least this, to not always react through a prism of old wounds. "Okay," I say. We chat a minute more then click off the line as Lidia goes back to whatever she was doing before I called.

~

I WALK FROM LIDIA's office toward the stairs, past the private dining room where one of the revelers recognizes me and calls out, "Professor McCanus." He's a skinny bean, all arms and legs, his suit silver, his hair cut neatly, moussed and made to stand in a way that doesn't quite work and yet is expensively styled and oddly perfect. I don't place him at first. He says my name again, calls out, "McCanus," reminds me who he is and invites me into the party.

I'm introduced to the rest of the room as the author of *Kilwater Speaks* and instantly everyone applauds. Being cheered for a book I wrote years ago is an odd little nut. I try repaying the compliment just the same, understand the expectations of my minor fame, and look to offer something clever, a witticism as is anticipated from a once-lauded author. Failing at this, I remain another few minutes, talk among those gathered, drink one of my beers, and hand off the other before making my exit while saying, "Cheers, folks. I hope you enjoyed the bar mitzvah." I've no idea what this means but everyone laughs.

I go back down to the bar, sit for a time, and try to decide what to do with the rest of my night. I'm imagining Gloria at her gig when I see two people from the party coming down the stairs. A man and woman, she in a lime-colored chiffon dress, sleeveless with the hem cut above the knee, and he in a gray silk suit, white shirt, and yellow tie drawn up tight to his neck. The woman has long black hair, is quite beautiful, Asian American, slender framed with a silhouette of curves. She descends the stairs in front of the man, swats at his hand each time he reaches for her.

I watch them pass through the restaurant and head outside where they stop and argue in front of the window. He seems to be entreating her while she keeps her hands moving as if her fingers are on fire. He straightens his shoulders, turns his frame into an exclamation point. As he does so, she gives her head a shake and points for him to go.

Once he disappears she comes back into the restaurant where, spotting me at the bar, she takes the seat next to me and orders a drink. "You saw that?"

"No," I answer.

"Liar," the woman smiles, and I see she has impressively white teeth. Of the man outside she says, "Some people are just *manuke*. You know *manuke*?"

"I assume it doesn't mean warm and cuddly."

She laughs at this, explains how the man had waited until they were out with friends to tell her that he's been offered a job in LA. "He expects me to be happy."

"For him?"

"For us. He wants me to go with him, expects me to just pick up and go."

"And you don't want to go?"

"Of course I don't want to go. Mostly though I don't like being told I should want to go and being blindsided by the whole thing."

"Right." I check her ring finger, see that she is married, and suspect her reaction to her husband's news is more complicated than simply not wanting to move. In this sort of discord there tends to be larger issues at play. She samples her drink then says in reference to meeting me upstairs, "You're probably enjoying this. All you writers love the drama."

"I don't know if that's true," I reply. "I enjoy writing about the drama but watching it for real is a more perverse pleasure."

This time when she laughs she touches my wrist. Her drink has a lime to match her dress. She empties her glass. I offer to buy her another, signal the bartender, and get two of the same. I think about Lidia and the friability of marriage, how ridiculous it is for me to be flirting here in Lidia's restaurant, and yet I am living now with Gloria and Lidia's reaction doesn't matter should she somehow hear of me at the bar. I say to the woman, "You don't have to tell me about your marriage." I find the best devise for getting people to talk is to come at things sideways and make it seem I have no real interest. "Your situation is private. We all have our issues."

"But that's the thing." She thanks me for the fresh drink, squeezes her lime, explains to me about the man with whom she was quarrelling, "He's not my husband."

"Well now." Who can guess these things? I lean closer and say, "So you're deciding whether or not to leave your husband for this other guy?"

Again she looks at me in a way I don't expect, as if I have said something stupid, her face pinched as she answers, "Why would I do that?"

"Because your boyfriend is leaving, because he asked you to go with him."

"And you think that's why I'm upset?"

"I think his asking has thrown a wrench into your perfect world."

She nods her head, holds her glass out for me to click my drink against. The second drink, on top of whatever she had upstairs, has her slightly drunk and from this she tells me, "I'm upset because he never should have asked me."

"Ahh."

"Lovers, right?"

"Manuke."

"Exactly. They're so presumptuous."

"You'd think they'd know their place."

"What about having an affair suggests I want a relationship?"

Oh this woman. I have my hand nearly on her leg now as I answer, "It suggests the opposite."

"It screams the opposite."

"You agree to a casual bump and tug."

"And the next thing you know they expect you to move across the country with them."

"It's crazy."

"I am married." She runs the edge of her glass across her lower lip.

I go ahead and tell her about the circumstance of my marriage and my current living arrangement, all of which she seems pleased to learn and says, "Then you understand."

"Of course I do."

"So." She puts her glass back on the bar, slides her knee next to mine, and with a conspiratorial invite asks, "Are we going to talk all night or what?"

CHAPTER FOUR

THREE DAYS LATER, CARA calls my cell. It's late afternoon and I'm coming from a meeting at the university. As part of my duties, as I teach very little these days, I agreed to sit on committees. Four years ago our department received a grant from the Zell Foundation and today we spent a few hours going over a list of this year's candidates to invite for readings.

Cara says she can meet me at my place at five. I nearly tell her that I changed my mind, that the project is a bit too big for me to take on this summer and perhaps next year is better. This seems reasonable, but then reasonableness is not much involved with what I'm doing lately. In the last few days, I have continued to carve out a plot, have come up with a way to ingratiate myself further, to see if I can't be introduced to both Cara and Matt and from there view them close-up together. My desire to see them interacting in conversation and not simply walking through the market is important, I tell myself, in order to better observe the fissures in their relationship, the cracks, as it were, into which I might stick my fingers and agitate a bit.

Gloria is out when I get home. I go upstairs and retrieve one of Matt's poetry collections, bring it down, and put it on the kitchen table. After this, I go out front and wait. Cara pulls up promptly at five and I walk her around the backyard where we spend half an hour discussing the project. I find her easy to talk with, intelligent and creative, confident and professional with an ability to take my crude ideas and make sense of them. She gives me prices to review, a timeframe to consider, and offers to draw up a detailed plan for a hundred dollars, which I will own even if I decide not to use her going forward. I agree to this, insist on writing her a check in good faith. We head inside where Cara notices the book by Matt on the kitchen table. I give her a moment then ask, "Do you know him?"

As they have different last names there's no way to suspect I've any knowledge, and then she tells me, "He's my husband."

I react with tremendous surprise. "Well now, well now," I exclaim. "Small world. Isn't that something? What a talented couple." I comment further, say how brilliant I find Matt's work, go ahead and quote the few lines I have purposely memorized from Matt's book. Cara's impressed, appreciates this, and when I say that a poet of Matt's obvious talent should be a beacon blazing across the scene, Cara replies with the slightest of shrugs, just enough for me to notice as she answers that Matt follows his own drummer beat and isn't very good at self-promotion.

I say that I am certain for Matt it's only a matter of time, and of course I would be happy to help, and here Cara surprises me in turn, reaches somewhat sheepishly into the knit satchel she carries and pulls out a copy of *Kilwater Speaks*. "I haven't read it," she admits. "But Matt's a fan." It seems she has mentioned my name to her husband, and asks if I'd sign the book, "To Matthew," she says then changes her mind and has me go with Matt.

~

YEARS FROM NOW, I will write:

In the summer, after Cara has left for SunGreen, and the kids, too, off to their summer jobs, Matt stretches and heads to the high school, where he runs sprints with the boys working out in the offseason with their teams. He joins the soccer team in their fitness drills and lifts weights with the footballers, exposing in the process his physical-self life's natural dichotomy. He challenges the boys and asks them to consider if the poet-man can run and bench with the best of them, what else might each of them do that they may not have imagined before?

Back home he showers, eats, and then writes. He is working on the start of a longer poem, something he's never tried before, book-length if the narrative holds. He starts with: *On the fruit tree / berries / I know the taste / and stain / if I bite too hard / with the front of my teeth. / There is this to deal with / the permanence / of what spills from inside.*

When Cara comes home he takes the book she brought for him, now signed, and examines the signature. The hand is loose and light, the *E* and the *M* opening like a bird in flight. She tells him then how she found his own book on the table, and how cool Matt thinks it is that a writer such as Eric McCanus is reading him. How flattering to be sure. She watches him holding the book like a prize, sees how happy he is and how much she wishes he took a similar joy in presenting his own work. In all the years they've been together, he's done but a handful of readings, hides from the invitations he receives, prizes and letters from other poets applauding his work. Somehow he is opposed to this, his ambition limited to the process of putting words on the page, as if doing more involves a vanity he refuses to possess.

She believes differently; she subscribes to the necessity of assertion and wishes he would champion his work and demand the world take note. How is it he can be so content to write as long and as well as he does with such little attention? Happiness has an odd effect on him, makes him tranquil and merrily resigned and he agrees, says he is happy and content with his life. She respects his ease and egoless manner, and yet sometimes she thinks his attitude is wearisome and an excuse to not challenge himself further. *Other men don't do this,* she thinks. *Other men know better.*

He is about to put the signed *Kilwater Speaks* up on the shelf when she stops him, tells him to wait, "I want to read it."

~

THE NEXT TIME CARA phones, I'm on my way to Colossal. She has completed a preliminary draft of the work I described for my yard and wants to show me. I say that I can stop by SunGreen if that's convenient. She is leaving shortly for a jobsite, however, so I propose meeting for lunch tomorrow. Cara suggests the Landmark Café. I agree and say, "It's a date."

As a gesture, during the meeting at my house, I give Cara the copy of Matt's book for him to sign. The act is intended to ingratiate myself further as I hardly care about the signature. At lunch Cara presents me with Matt's book. I act well pleased, examine the signed page, the design of the M and the G given a tight cursive set on the title page. "How wonderful," I say. "How generous."

Cara wears a clean sweatshirt over her work clothes, her hair brushed back, her face and hands washed clean of the morning's project. We don't talk about the garden right away, speak of other things first. I ask and Cara tells me about her family, her son Eli, Defender of Man, and daughter Lia, Bearer of Good News. She liked the names, she says, even before knowing their meaning. I tell her that I don't have kids, that it is something I think about from time to time and have actually once put a great deal of effort into pursuing. She finds this funny, and I smile.

The plans for the yard are sketched across several large sheets of drafting paper, rolled up and held together by a thick elastic band. Cara unrolls the sheets across the table and shows me her design. Her handiwork is impressive, containing all the details as we had earlier discussed. I listen while she explains what I am seeing. The final page is an elaborate computerized rendering of what the project will look like when complete. "It's quite beautiful," I say and then confide about the garden, "It's for my girlfriend. And my wife. My ex-wife. It's something I hope they both like."

Cara finds the statement strange and I reply, "It's a strange situation. Honestly, if I invested this much energy trying to make Lidia happy while we were married, who knows?"

"And your girlfriend?"

"Yes, well," I say, "she's not actually my girlfriend. We're living together but we're not really together, if that makes sense. Plus I'm trying hard not to fall in love with her."

"You're living with her but trying not to fall in love?"

"Right."

Cara has a soft face, a pillowy full moon, and when not concentrating on work her expression becomes something almost tender. Hoping to further gain her trust, sharing these personal truths, I say of my feelings for Gloria, "I honestly don't know. I've written two books and a bunch of stories and songs, and every relationship in them is just me floundering around trying to figure things out." I do what I can to make myself sound sincere.

Cara notices and says, "I saw that in *Kilwater*. Your characters really do try."

"I thought you hadn't read my book."

"I hadn't before."

Our food comes and we eat. I keep our conversation moving in the direction I want, reminding Cara that I wrote *Kilwater* some time ago. "I think I got lucky. Back then I didn't know yet what I didn't know yet."

Cara smiles as I say this. Her smile is also warm, not flirtatious, but kind and attentive to what I am saying. "Youth allows us to be fearless," she says and I agree.

"In an odd way," I tell her, "getting older narrows rather than expands our scope, allows experience to chip away at us, forces us emotionally and creatively to feel safer and more content with what we know." I state this then add, "In terms of art I mean. And love."

Cara says she will have to hear more first because "contentment is a complicated condition. I mean, we seek it and at the same time have to be careful not to become static."

"That's exactly true." I like the way she is quick to argue. No bullshit with her. I answer that of course she's right but that "when we're younger, contentment is the most distant sort of abstraction while experience is something we acquire but don't yet have. We write from the heart and fall in love the same way. We have no skill or practice so we jump right in and what we produce is raw and honest and sometimes, if we're lucky, we make it work."

I tell her how I miss those days, that I haven't published a book in years, can barely get my head around what I am trying to create, and I think this was in part because all of my experiences cluttered and clanged against my effort. "If that makes sense. I miss the unknown," I say. "I need something to get me charged up."

"You mean something to believe in?"

"Believe in. That's it exactly." I am pleased to hear her say this. "My problem is my belief system is off. I've spent a good long while trying to write what I believe but I'm not convinced anymore that I believe in anything, or more that what I believe isn't completely wrong, and when I try to explain it in my writing it falls away like so much ash from a smoldering stick. This scares me and is the problem I've been having." I am jumping around a bit with my thoughts, but have in mind a place

I want to wind up. I compare writing to marriage, say that in both we start with a narrative in mind, a direction we want to take our story, and then things happen to throw us off. "With a novel, when the writing is going well, I can follow the direction my narrative wants to take me, I can identify the internal needs of the book, the real story, which, should I miss and try to create something else, the entire work will collapse if I don't see what I've done wrong and get back on track.

"Relationships are the same," I zero in then. "They have their own internal compass we can't always control. We may love one another and still make a mess of things, become clumsy or blind, overburdened or complacent in time, develop resentment, suffer through episodes of boredom, indifference, and worse."

"But that's only natural." Cara takes my comment and goes with it this way. "It's not that things change but how we deal with them that matters."

"You're right." I have her talking, and answer, "Dealing with things is key. But dealing with them is different from feeling about them and reacting to them as we once did. Experience teaches us how to accept what we can no longer have. With writing, we develop technique and style, learn how to maneuver our words even when inspiration fails us. We forget how we were able to approach the blank page with nothing but desire and come instead to rely on a more tempered talent. With relationships," I continue, "we do the same, we learn how to manage one another long after we can no longer remember how or why we fell in love."

"That's too harsh." She wastes no time challenging my claims. "All relationships require the necessity of adjustment."

"Require, sure," I repeat the phrase then ask, "but aren't the adjustments we make an acknowledgment that something's wrong? As we get older we become more adept at self-delusion. If you think about it, the best thing experience does is teach us how to perform emotional sleight of hand."

"Now I know you're kidding."

"But I'm not."

"Then you're a cynic."

"Am I?" I haven't realized fast enough that I am actually making her mad, and still I say, "I'm sure there are things about Matt that disappoint you."

"Experience is a gift." She ignores my comment, is defensive here, and replies, "Nothing stays the same. As a writer, you can't write the same way now as you did when you were twenty-five and no one would want you to. It wouldn't be honest. I think it's the same thing with relationships. Experience lets us know we love someone. The fact that things change is not always a bad thing. Adjusting to change requires acceptance not self-delusion. That relationships go through permutations allows us to change together and through that change become closer." She ends this way, picks up her BLT, and asks, "But how did we get on this?"

"You read my book."

She gives a nod, her head tipping just an inch or so to the side as she teases, "That was my mistake."

"Yes," I smile again, different than before, and tell her, "It definitely was."

CHAPTER FIVE

FTER LUNCH I GO to Colossal where I have a session scheduled with a band called Render to Caesar (RTC). RTC is four guys with a loose Blind-Melon-meets-R.E.M. sound they can't quite bring together. It's easy to apply a conventional fix and call it a day, but instead I tell the band to take the song they've brought me and riff on it. "Let's go off the edges," I say. "Give me some Wilco, give me some Allman Brothers, some Dave Matthews when he really lets go. I don't want any Goddamn Dead," I say, "but wouldn't mind if you want to work in some Phish." After all these years I have no technical way of explaining what I want any better than this. Occasionally I will play my guitar, or piano, but I am only a marginal musician and am better at using my words. My routine has not changed much over the years. I stand with my back turned as the band plays, and when I like what I hear I give further instruction.

Frankie, our engineer, records the session so we have something to play back. I tweak the chorus, move the vocals, demonstrate where verses should appear, and show how to stretch the instrumentation. The singer's a beast and I intend to use his voice as a tease throughout, make listeners anticipate the lyric's return. We spend four hours expanding a three-minute song into a seven-minute-and-thirty-second anthem. The band soars, demonstrates a greater command of their gifts when allowed to play without constraint. Now trusting and willing to follow me, we create a one-off piece I expect will surprise Geffen Records, which has RTC under contract; the tune is four minutes too long to get radio play anywhere other than the alt college stations and late-night FM feeds, and still when we finish the band is ecstatic and knows exactly what we have made.

After high fives and a few shots of WhistlePig to celebrate, I head home. Gloria is watching TV in the front room. On the screen is one of those ubiquitous cop shows where good-looking thirty-somethings solve matters of espionage all over the globe. Here I see a couple wearing evening dress being chased down a beach in what appears to be Morocco. "Which one are you watching?" I ask.

Gloria replies, "I'm not sure."

She has worked a shift at Danny's and has no plans for tonight. I tell her about my session with RTC and then about my lunch with Cara. Gloria knows now that I've been in touch with Cara, has given me grief about the garden, is amused by my persistence, and says, "I want to meet them."

I laugh at the idea. Gloria mutes the TV, turns in her chair and asks, "What's so funny?"

I answer, "I don't think Cara and Matt will know what to make of you."

"There's nothing to make."

"Yeah, well I'm sure you'll meet Cara when she starts in on the yard."

"Did you tell her about me?" Gloria asks.

I answer, "Yes."

"What did you say?"

"I said that we are living together but not in a relationship. I told her I was having the garden made for you and for Lidia."

"You told her the garden was for both of us?"

"I explained the situation."

Gloria points at my head and says, "The situation is all in there, McCanus."

"Maybe so."

"And are you?"

"Am I what?"

"Having the garden made for me and Lidia?"

"Sure. Yes, I am." I would like to think Gloria would prefer I hadn't included Lidia in my story but more probably she doesn't really care. Gloria never minds when I talk about Lidia. She doesn't complain when I tell her about other women. I have told her about the woman at the bar and this was fine. Our relationship, such as it is, relies on equanimity and causing no harm. Here, however, she seems to be egging me on, wants to know what good a garden is to Lidia when she no longer lives here?

I reply, "Some connections run deep forever, no matter, you know?"

Gloria stares at me now as if my answer's all wrong and there's something else she wants to say. She is wearing the cut-off sweats she likes to sleep in, a sleeveless top, her hair finger-brushed up. I let her stare then finally say, "What?"

She sighs and goes, "Nothing," clicks off the TV and leaves the room. I get something to eat from the kitchen, then go upstairs and fall asleep in the guest room. Gloria doesn't come get me. At some point I wake with a start, try and place where I am, and find myself breathing hard in a state of near hyperventilation as I can't quite be sure if I've been dreaming or whether I did in fact just tell Gloria that I love her. *Hell. Hell. Of course not, McCanus.* What foolish things come into my head when I least expect them.

~

THE NEXT MORNING I write:

Together they sit in the front room and watch a program on TV. The actors are handsome, B-list performers, as interchangeable as dress socks. The show presents the couple in dinner attire, carrying out some sort of skullduggery before being chased down a beach. After a time, Cara gets up and moves to the couch, lies down and thinks about her lunch with McCanus. She recalls her reaction to reading *Kilwater Speaks*, how she found the characters in the novel filled with an unrelenting, bumble-footed energy, a flaunting of the human spirit as a way of saying, *Hell yes I'm alive and what of it?*

All of this is different from Matt's poems, which are more mellifluous in their offering. If she had to point to something that has worn thin for her in Matt's work, if she were forced to do so, it would be the consistent way his voice contained a sense of mournful cheer, as if finding the beauty in the struggle was life's single most important calling rather than embracing beauty and being sorry separately for what they truly were.

She closes her eyes on the couch. He lets her sleep a bit before waking her. While she sleeps, he reads. When she wakes, she thanks him for letting her rest. He goes back to his book, catches her once and then again staring at him. "What?" he finally asks.

"Nothing," she answers.

He interprets this all wrong, tells her then, "I love you."

She smiles as she must and says, "What things come into your head when I least expect them."

~

Two DAYS AFTER OUR lunch, Cara lets me know she has a better sense of her schedule and anticipates the project in front of mine being completed by the end of the week. She gives me a date she can start on the yard and has already asked me to review the specific plants and trees available for the garden as she needs to order some of the deciduous trees soon. I tell her that I am partial to the cherry and plum mixed with evergreens. "While I have you," I say. "I've been thinking."

I take my cell outside and stand on the deck looking at the backyard as Fred runs about. This morning, while I wrote, I decided to rework the start of my novel. I've done this now more times than I can count though here, rather than force the issue of love's insubstantiality, I set the stage differently. Instead of beginning with the husband's cuckolding, I chose to make the couple unaware of their impending vulnerability, allowing the action to proceed as if by accident, proving through each scene that love is a vagary, as impermanent as a match flame. My intent was to do this not cynically, as Cara accused me at lunch, not with a loutish yowl, but rather with a commiserative approach, which demonstrated a certain sympathy to the inevitability of love's collapse.

I ask Cara if she is familiar with the Zell Readings and she says yes. I had hoped for this. The reading series is tremendously popular. I remind her of my position at the university, explain how the Zell provides us with funding to bring writers to campus in order to share their work with an appreciative audience. I let her know the university rarely selects a local writer, that we try and avoid any homegrown prejudice and internal complications, but since Matt isn't affiliated with the university, since he's a poet and not a novelist—as novelists are more pissy about such things—as the university hasn't once had a local author awarded a Zell, and as I'm a fan and my vote carries weight, "I would like to nominate Matt."

Cara does not know what to say—she is overwhelmed by my offer. I describe what will happen if Matt is chosen, how he will draw national attention, will receive a stipend, will be brought in to do a few events on campus beyond his reading, class talks and workshops and such. There will be a luncheon and dozens of new reviews as the Zell is quite the prize. "What do you think?" I ask Cara, conspiring to have it seem as though we are deciding together.

When she replies, "Yes, of course. How wonderful," I say I should probably speak with Matt as well, get to know him a bit better and would she mind if I give him a call?

I get Matt's phone number and put it in my cell. It will take considerable effort on my part to get the committee to sign off on using one of the four yearly stipends for a local poet of no real repute, but for now the outcome is not the issue. "Happy to do it," I say, "For Matt."

Cara thanks me again, and does as I hoped she might: invites me to dinner. I remain eager to see them in their natural habitat, to visit with them more intimately at their home and I accept her invitation at once.

~

I CALL MATT THAT evening. Now that we have exchanged signed copies of our books, I speak to him chummily, carrying on as if we're old friends. I flatter him as I explain about the Zell, fill him in as Cara has waited for me to break the news. Startled, he goes quiet, knows of course about the Zell and its authors and says of my nominating him, "It's very kind of you."

I hesitate just half a beat before replying, "Really, Matt, it isn't."

~

THE NEXT DAY I leave Colossal by five, stop on my way home to purchase a bottle of Dewar's, then wash up and change my shirt. Gloria is heading out to play music with friends. When I tell her about my plans for the evening she follows me upstairs, stands in the doorway, and asks, "What are you up to, McCanus?"

The walls of my bedroom are painted an off shade of green. A fresh coat was added just before Lidia and I separated, as she felt we needed. I answer Gloria by insisting it's only a dinner, though when questioned as to what prompted the invitation I tell her about the Zell. Gloria tips herself back from the shoulders as if my news requires more room for her to take in. She walks to my closet, nixes the shirt I have chosen, and selects another. "So let's see," she says, "you've hired Cara to build a garden and now you're getting her husband a Zell, but you're not up to anything?"

"Nope." I change my shirt again and do not attempt to explain, I know better than to say Matt's poems inspired me and that my gesture's sincere.

Gloria stands in front of me and fixes the collar on my shirt. Her hair is longer than it was when we first met, the coloring a half-shade lighter, she wears it today pulled into a puff at the back of her head. After eight months I am fully aware that Gloria is smarter than me about most things, and still I refuse to take her seriously as she cautions me and says, "You know this is going to end badly, don't you?"

"I don't know that. And there is no *this.*"

She slides her hands down my arms and steps away to look at me. I have brushed my hair and put on the blue shirt Gloria's chosen. On the underside of Gloria's right arm she has tattooed in black ink the phrase: *The map is not the territory*. I like that she has inked this there, find the tattoo sexy. For a moment I want to kiss her, am close enough to do so—proximity always significant for me. I button my shirt as Gloria watches. Shaking her head, she says in summary, "You're not going to learn anything about their marriage by screwing with them. There isn't a relationship in the world that can't be fucked with."

This is true, I suppose, and still I continue to claim, "I'm not up to anything. I'm getting to know them is all. That's the worst you can accuse me of."

Gloria goes again to my closet. I've carved out space for her, given her a handful of hangers, a shelf, and two drawers in my bureau. She changes her clothes, pulls off her T-shirt and jeans, selects a light summer dress, an off shade of orange, and slips it on like a fresh skin and frees her hair. I watch her dress; I think at first she is changing in order to have me take her to dinner, though seeing my concern she tells me not to worry. "I told you, I'm playing with friends tonight." She smiles at this, a half-tick ahead of me before she says, "You, too, it seems, McCanus."

~

IN THE BEDROOM, I write:

He watches her dress. Downstairs the table is set, the salad made, the water for the corn placed to boil, the chicken and potatoes put in the oven. She undresses and dresses again. He witnesses each transformation. The walls of their bedroom are jade, in need of fresh paint. He hasn't noticed this before now. He wears a tan shirt with rolled-up sleeves, wants to remain in shorts but she has him put on a pair of slacks instead. He stands in the center of the room and she fixes his collar. As a caution, as she can't help, excited as she is, looking forward to the evening, she reminds him of the opportunity presented. He is aware, but prefers not to take things as seriously, he is less anxious than she, the stakes not so much a concern for him. He answers this way, jokes about the fortuity of chance encounters, then tells her not to worry and what's the worst that can happen?

~

I PARK ON THE street, forget the Dewar's, and have to go back to my car. Matt opens the front door as I'm coming up the walk and we shake hands. He is shorter than me by an inch or so, is casually dressed in slacks and a shirt, somewhat more preppy than as I saw him before at the market. For no reason I slap his shoulder. Although we are roughly the same age I say, "Matthew, my boy," and present him with the whiskey.

We go into the front room. Cara comes from the kitchen, hand extended to greet me. Changed from her work clothes, her shorts and T-shirt, wearing a cotton sundress, a white and blue print, sleeveless, her hair combed into a frizzy off-red frame around her face, which is treated now to a light touch of blush and eyeliner, she is a handsome figure, not beautiful but something nearly better. I take her hand then lean in and kiss her cheek. I have learned from years of attending events—parties and readings, conferences and banquets—that a kiss establishes the right climate. I'm taken on a tour of the house, shown the library and the room where Matt writes, and brought outside where we stand on the deck and look at the yard Cara has designed with angled beds of perennials: heuchera and butterfly weed, summer wine and bladdernut.

Drinks are served in the front room. Matt joins me for whiskey while Cara has poured herself some wine. We talk for a time about nothing in particular, about their kids and the warmth of the summer, about my work at Colossal, which they seem now to know about, too. Matt says he's a fan of Jhene Aiko and Grace Mitchell, both of whom I've worked with, while Cara goes back and forth to the kitchen, checks our meal, calls out that she's a big John Mayer fan and have I ever met him?

We talk about Matt's poems and about the Zell, discuss my writing, and what I'm working on now. I say that I am trying to get through a proper draft of a new novel and when Matt asks what it's about, I answer, "It's a love story."

Soon dinner is ready and we eat in the dining area. The walls and floor and table are composed of dark woods, a brown and black print by Klee on the main wall. Cara and Matt sit beside one another while I am on the opposite side of the table, directly across from them. I ask Cara questions about her work, her influences and most challenging projects. I tell her that I am excited about my garden and praise again the design she's created for me. We talk a bit more about Matt's work, discuss for a time the poetry of Elizabeth Bishop, her recurrent theme an examination of childhood and our exile from Eden and our struggle to address external forces, the grief and longing that life throws at us. Matt embraces the subject eagerly; he believes the purpose of poetry is to create a verbal vision of the world as a beautiful jungle, both violent and cruel, generous and forgiving. Cara jokes of Matt's determination to reduce even the most vile experiences into a thing of wonder, and how his favorite line is from Bishop's poem "First Death in Nova Scotia." "*Arthur's coffin was / A little frosted cake.* Which for dessert," Cara laughs, "I won't be serving."

Matt laughs at this as well. Together this way I find nothing different from what I saw at the market, see only an adoring and supportive couple and maybe Gloria was right about keeping my distance and not fucking with them. *Here is who they are,* I am tempted to concede, though not quite yet, I am reminded of how Cara shrugged at lunch when discussing Matt's ambitions and think maybe her comment now about Matt's poetry wasn't quite as innocent as it seemed, and, calculating still, I ask myself how am I supposed to get beyond the surface shine and down to hidden truths if I don't rattle cages?

"Let me ask you something." Halfway through our meal, as we are discussing again the ability of great poets to explore the world in all its varied shades, I raise my fork and compose one of those open-ended riddles, with implications on either side, as I say to Matt, "If you could have one but not both, if you could write a transcendent poem, something singular and original enough to make the gods weep, or you could have a love affair that would define your heart forever and rally you like Catherine and Grigory beneath the starry, starry nights, which would you choose?"

Matt answers at once, sure of his reply, and doesn't have to think as he says, "But it's not a question. If you insist on an answer there's only one."

"Which is?"

"Love, of course."

"Love and not art?"

"You asked for one," Matt confirms.

"So you would give up your art for love?"

"Under your scenario. Hypothetically."

"That's interesting," I say and look at Cara. "That's revealing."

"Love is the ambition of all poets," Matt nearly blushes as he says this, his cheeks in a spasm of twitches.

I hide my pleasure at his use of the word "ambition" and reply that artists forever, and poets in particular, have written about unrequited love, about lost love, about the want and desire of love without having love. Matt agrees with me but says, "That isn't what you asked. You wanted to know which I would choose."

"And you would choose love over your art?"

"Of course. If there's only one choice," Matt repeats, "for purposes of discussion, if you're after only one then I would choose love." He stares at me, does not look at Cara as he speaks, assumes she already knows this would be his answer. I check Cara again for her reaction but so far she resists showing me anything. I consider drawing her directly into the debate then decide this would be a mistake. Better to be patient and let things unfold. I continue and say with brash dispatch, "Not me. If faced with the question of which comes first, an artist must understand art is the only answer."

"I don't agree." Matt explains, "Art is a pursuit, an attempt to expose the world in its every permutation, while love is the actuality of living the fullest sort of life. Why would an artist surrender the greatest gift life has to offer in order to write about the very thing they've rejected?"

"Because they're an artist," I answer at once. "Because that's what it means to have real ambition."

Matt laughs as if I have said something amusing. "That's artist-speak," he tells me. "That's egoistic indulgence. Being happy is the purpose of life," he says exactly as Gloria.

I argue the point, insisting, "Happiness is a complicated ambition, Matt, especially for an artist. Love is not the sole form of happiness. Producing great art is, for the real artist, the highest form of being. In order to create great art one must be completely selfish and sacrificing and can't be distracted by love."

"Distracted by…?" Matt repeats the phrase as if he is startled and can't quite believe I have said this. "Love is not a distraction." He seems almost hurt. "An artist can't push his heart aside in order to write a better sonnet or novel about the very thing they've just discarded."

"Of course they can. Without question they can. That's exactly what great artists do." I maintain my conviction.

Matt counters, "I don't believe that. It may appear that way to some, to those artists spurned by love, or failing at love, but if an artist actually no longer believed in love, if they felt that the prospect of love was forever out of reach, or were willing to displace love for their own ambition, they would be lost and unable to create a single piece of art. Without love there is nothing. To not believe in love, to lose faith, or diminish love's value, an artist would have nothing to say, his work would just be hollow. In that I'm certain."

I stare across the table and say, "Spoken like a poet." I mean this in jest but my tone suggests otherwise. Matt stiffens his shoulders while Cara looks at me from across the table. She has given us our moment but the topic seems to have made her uncomfortable. I think at first that she's inclined to agree with Matt but there is something in the way she glances between us that causes me to wonder if she hasn't found my argument more convincing. I'm curious to know what she's thinking, if she remembers our lunch and how we discussed the process of our own work. When I spoke of writing, my voice filled with a rare intensity, and she seemed to like that.

Perhaps she's thinking of this now as she drinks her wine and is considering the complications and how I've addressed them, how I fight the temptation to treat love like a religious calling, my passions antithetical to Matt's whose reverence toward love is more like a capitulation than a living breathing thing. Maybe this explains what happens next: as Matt continues to look at Cara, he is staring at her as I finish defending my view and the requirement of controlling the heart and not the other way around, while Matt replies with the sort of sentimentality that appears to embarrass Cara, as he says again that love is the endgame, selfless and singularly sustaining. He continues to stare at his wife, so tender and convinced that she can't help herself, she doesn't mean to, but she frowns mournfully, if only for a second, and, straining to recover, turns away.

CHAPTER SIX

L IDIA LIVES DOWNTOWN. SHE has rented a condo in the new Baywood Towers, fourteen stories above Seline Avenue with a panoramic view of the river. I leave Matt and Cara's on good terms, our conversation transitioning toward more neutral subjects; we talk about the need for rain, compare our sports allegiances, share local gossip, agree to disagree on the matter of love and art though express respect for the other's opinion. Driving home, I review again the way Matt reacted to my question, and how Cara looked in turn. I wonder what it all means and what I might have accomplished. Despite my firm denial, I can't help but envy Matt's defense of love, and, troubled by this, I text Lidia, tell her I'm stopping by.

I get no answer, but when I arrive and park at her building, the doorman ushers me in as Lidia instructed. I take the elevator to the fourteenth floor. Since our divorce I've been to Lidia's a handful of times. We are this, a divorced couple still in the process of figuring things out, learning how to engage and disengage like cats crossing a wire. Lidia is barefoot when she lets me in and the cool marble tiles catch her arch and occasionally squeak as she walks. She brings me into the front room where she sits on her couch. The couch is a Braxton, all the furniture modern. I head to the bar first, in want of a drink. Lidia tells me she is cutting back, trying not to drink late, but that I should have what I want. Words to live by. I find a bottle of Knob Creek, pour myself a shot, ask for news on her sous chef and Lidia says, "That meal is over." When I tell her I'm sorry, she calls me a liar and asks about Gloria.

I come to the couch. Lidia has changed from whatever dress she wore at Caber Hills tonight into shorts and a blue cotton shirt. I'm close enough to reach over and touch her leg but don't do this. Instead I update her on the garden, let her know I've hired Cara and that the conversion of the yard will be done this summer. "I just had dinner at Cara's house, in fact," I say, and mention that Cara's husband Matt is a poet I've been reading.

"Since when do you read poetry?"

Lidia knows my predilections better than anyone, and as I answer, "Lately. More since you left," she rolls her eyes, stretches her legs, and moves my shot glass with her foot. I tell her then about the conversation at dinner, how Matt's opinion of love clashed with mine, and eventually Cara's, and that this came as a relief.

"Why?"

"Because up until then they presented themselves as the perfect couple."

Lidia warns me not to start one of my half-drunken soliloquies but I pay no attention, remind her that she asked and go on to explain, "This marriage thing is juddering. I'm curious to understand how folks like Matt and Cara manage to stay together while you and I fell apart."

Lidia says, "We did not just fall apart, Eric. We took a leap and then we crashed."

I reply, "That's true, in part," but that the crash could have been avoided, did not need to be fatal.

Lidia disagrees, gets up and walks across the floor. Her condo has an open design and I can see her as she goes to her wet bar and fills a second glass with a shot of Knob Creek. She is a handsome woman, even more so I think than when we first met. Age agrees with her. At nearly forty, she embodies a confidence that is earned, her features set in fine detail, her body fuller now, her curves inviting, more so than the slender spunk of younger women. She stands behind the bar, gives thought to what she wants to say, and then begins. "I'm not blaming you," she makes reference to our marriage crashing.

The statement feels foreboding, implies forgiveness for a transgression she's already found me guilty of. Rather than ask what it is exactly I'm being absolved of, I say, "That's good. And I don't blame you."

"We're both responsible."

"In our own way, though you left me."

"I left you, Eric, because there was no reason to stay."

I listen from across the room, know I need to be careful as Lidia is sharper than I am and if I don't respect this, if I resort to banter and fail to pay attention to what is being said, she will eat me like toast. Lidia comes back to the couch and sits down. "Let's not fight," she says, and even before I can agree she goes on. "When we first met you were in a state. The publishing of *Kilwater* was too much for you and you were smart enough to know if you didn't find a way to ground yourself that you'd fall apart like Radiguet and Fournier before you turned thirty."

"Where is this going?"

"I needed you, too," she continues. "We used each other to confirm ourselves and that's okay. I liked it. I liked what we were doing," she says. "All of it. Having a partner who allowed me to be totally free was perfect for me. We let each other do our thing. We had our work, we partied together, gave each other permission to live as we pleased. It took me a long time to realize what we were doing wasn't the same thing."

She moves from the couch and sits on the coffee table directly in front of me. Her summary of our relationship is making me uneasy and I am in the process of disputing her claims when she asks, "Do you remember Gayle Hein?"

"Shit."

"Not shit."

"Why would you bring that up?"

"Because it's relevant."

"In what possible way?"

"You want to know why I left you."

"Because of Gayle? But that was years ago. And you were there."

"I was there, right. And you didn't want me there."

"I was uncomfortable with you watching," I tell her. "That's all."

Lidia says, "That's what I thought at first. But that's not it. It wasn't that you were uncomfortable with me watching, it was that you couldn't understand how I was happy for you. I wanted you to be happy. I loved you and as long as you were open with me, I was fine with almost anything. But your sense of freedom and mine were always two different things. You liked the idea of me being with someone else not because you wanted me to be happy the way I wanted you to be happy, but because you liked torturing yourself. Being troubled by love is what makes you feel alive."

"Christ."

"If you don't want to talk about this then don't ask me to explain why I left."

"Fine, okay," I say, though I can't resist adding, "I've always wanted you to be happy."

"That's rhetoric, Eric," Lidia dismisses. "That's comfort-speak. The truth is your sense of freedom is never as open as you claim."

"This is crazy." I get up once more, move past where Lidia is sitting on the table, grab my shot glass, and pour myself another drink. I begin to say all this analysis is useless, that I know perfectly well who I am and that I was always open with her and our relationship and was happy when she was happy and she should know that. "I was there for you," I say, that actions mean something and that the freedom and faith I extended validated us.

"But that's just it." She gives me the face I don't want to see, the one that is already sad for me and difficult to please. "Nothing we did validated us, it only confirmed how little you believed in us. Your sense of freedom and openness wasn't offered to make me happy, it was used to absolve yourself of responsibility. You used freedom not to be closer but to hold me off. You never wanted us to have an open relationship because you actually believed this was the truest way to love someone, you did it because you were too lazy to try and hold onto me. Loving someone is too hard for you, Eric. Too frightening and demanding."

"That's ridiculous. That's just not true. Lid, listen." From my vantage there appears to be three ways to play what is unfolding. I can lash out angrily in my defense and drive Lidia further away; I can laugh off her suggestion, make light of our situation, and hope that my ability to take none of this too seriously puts her enough at ease to maybe sleep with me; or I can attempt to get out in front of what she's saying and show her I understand. I weigh each option, choose the third and dive in with, "You're right, you're right."

"What am I right about, Eric?"

"I know what you're saying. It doesn't matter how a couple chooses to live as long as they live well together. I let you down, I know that. I should have been more open with my openness," I try and be clever with this. "I should have been okay and trusted that you wanted me to be happy. I should have enjoyed watching you. You would have known then that everything was okay. It's why I came by tonight," I try now to spin, to make sense of it all myself, the way Matt had championed love, and what would happen if I did so now with Lidia?

When Lidia says my name again, says *Eric* as if the word is a stone she is pushing from her tongue, I know that I haven't quite found the mark. She tells me, "It isn't about my watching or you watching, it's about believing absolutely in the things we do."

This is exactly what Gloria said, and once more I insist, "I do believe."

"But you don't, Eric. You can write down the words, create books and songs, but you don't believe any of it. I wouldn't have minded that either," she says, "if I thought all of this was coming from a point of strength. But you're not strong enough for that, Eric. You're really quite weak."

Lidia can be wicked when she wants. I feel my anger pushing past all manageable points and lash back, "Oh, so now we're resorting to insult. Now you're saying you're stronger than me."

"I am, Eric. And that's why I left."

"Because I'm weak?"

"And dishonest."

"Fuck." I can't help myself now and begin to bark, "Hell, Lid. I have loved you bravely and completely and if you can't see that, if you don't realize, then I'm sorry."

Lidia is still sitting on the edge of the table facing me across the room. I flip things around, resort to saying that she's the one who doesn't understand how fragile love is, how no love lasts, that even Matt and Cara, even a couple as stout and determined as they are can be wedged apart if the circumstance presents itself, and what Lidia needs to concentrate on is not how I disappointed her but my willingness to try again. "Love is about adaptability," I argue here, say as Cara at lunch the other day. "It's about necessary adjustments and how willing I am to try."

"You only want to try, Eric, because I'm already gone. You should try with Gloria."

"But I don't love Gloria."

"Yes, you do. You know you do and that scares you, too. Stop fighting it, Eric." Lidia gets up and walks past me toward the door. Her face is completely neutral now, nearly to the point of disinterest, which is hurtful in an altogether different way. "Let's end this," she says. "Let's not say anything else tonight."

I start to reply but catch myself, I know saying anything further would just get Lidia mad, and, turning my shot glass over for dramatic effect, I nod several times as if this will convince me, heave a sigh, tell Lidia, "All right then," follow her to the door, and say goodnight.

CHAPTER SEVEN

IN THE KITCHEN, AFTER their guest is gone, Matt helps Cara clean up. She is silent now, and when he asks if she's okay, she pauses a moment then smiles unconvincingly and turns away.

In bed, he lies beside her, waiting for her to sleep. The house is quiet. The kids have come home and are now asleep. He thinks back to dinner, thinks about the things said and not said, thinks of the way she looked and how she didn't intend for him to see. She doesn't drift off as fast as usual tonight, but stirs instead and reaches for his hand. He gives himself a moment to understand. Most times when they make love she is playful, laughs at the exchange, at how good it feels and how ridiculous this thing they do is, how much she enjoys it and will chuckle in the middle before going somewhere else, somewhere inside herself, as he is, warm and marveled. Tonight her reaching for him is different, conveys a want for clarity in their exchange.

He goes to her, follows her lead, lets her kiss him, touch him, and ask to be touched. He does so until she is ready and then he slides on top, slides inside. She is quiet, much more so than usual. He gives her exactly and only what she seems to need, kisses her neck and shoulders and ears softly until he shivers and comes. She clings to him afterward, still silent, still not saying a word. He thinks she is okay, but when he finally moves off, there in the dark, to his side of the bed, he can hear her, catches her as she delivers the soft exhale of someone almost unrecognizable and far from at peace.

CHAPTER EIGHT

GLORIA WORKS THE EARLY shift at Danny's. The house feels different when she's not here. I spend the morning trying to compose a scene about my couple in bed coming to terms with what they can't quite figure out or confess in anything more than sighs and whispers. The scene is hard. I keep thinking of what Lidia said last night, how she accused me of not believing in love and what sort of nonsense? If I didn't believe, how could I doubt?

I finish writing and come downstairs, go into the kitchen, stand facing the window, and look out at the yard. The day is clear and I have to squint in order to see a trace of cloud. I think once more about Matt and Cara and our conversation at dinner, and feel that I am making progress, that I am on the verge of proving how all couples are brittle and essentially the same; I do not entertain any thoughts of relinquishing my plan, I am determined despite Gloria's caution, and to prove as much I find my phone and call Matt.

He is replacing the brick in his garden wall, he tells me. Reinforcing what needs repair. Eli has the day off and is helping Matt now. Together they mix the mortar and level each row. On the phone, I thank Matt for dinner and let him know everything with the Zell is progressing nicely, that it won't be long, and why don't we meet for drinks soon and go over the details? We decide on Wednesday at five, agree on Bachman's. I end the call by wishing Matt well.

I make several more calls that afternoon. Everyone on the Zell committee receives a follow-up pitch from me, my endorsement of Matt is confirmed, and what a great favor I would take it as if they could see their way clear to voting for our local prodigy. I've been invited to read in New York and fly out the next morning. Although I haven't published a book in years, there are stores still interested in having me, and my appearance at the Strand draws a nice crowd. I present a chapter from *Kilwater* where my protagonist is at a party and winds up accidently insulting the wife of a city councilman. *Who knew she wasn't pregnant? How was I supposed to tell?* Such a funny scene, right? People at readings always want to be amused.

I go out for drinks afterward with a handful of writers I know in the city. We are a convivial group, we become loud when brought together, joke freely, make light of one another's work and reviews, both good and bad. I head back to my hotel with one of the writers, a woman I know less than the others. She has just published a collection of stories, claims to have met me twice before but I don't recall.

Gloria phones as the woman is dressing to leave my hotel. It is one in the morning and I have asked the front desk to get her a cab. I've been thinking about Lidia, and Gloria, thinking about their happiness, about my happiness, about getting laid tonight and what it means. I think about conquests and carrying on, about the point of it all, which is a fool's question really, and then I ask Gloria why she is calling.

I do this in a tender voice, I am not accusing or complaining but hoping her reason is that she's been missing me even though I refuse to say I've been missing her. In the past, during sex, my level of concentration is heightened by the fact that I am fucking someone new in a setting steeped with adventure, where the promiscuity excites me. Tonight, however, I noticed a definite decline in my delivery, my thoughts adrift, and I had to reapply my concentration, request certain verbal commitments from my partner, divert myself from the diversion as it were until the deed was done.

"Are you alone?" Gloria, too, uses a tender voice when she asks. I tell her yes, and this is true, in every way but one. The woman blows me kisses from the door.

"Liar," Gloria says, and this is also an accurate assessment.

~

My flight out of La Guardia the next day is delayed and I don't land until late. Gloria is asleep when I get home. I use the bathroom then go into the bedroom and approach the bed. The drapes are parted just slightly and across the bed is a sliver of moon. I see Gloria there in the light, rolled onto her side, her features in profile clear, a sort of three-dimensional silhouette laid out on the white of her pillow, her hair in flow, her left arm atop the sheet, her legs beneath wrapped around another pillow between her knees. It is a mistake, I know, but I am thinking once more about what Lidia said, about who I love and should love, about courage and fear, weakness and strength. I am tired and vulnerable and all these thoughts and deeds have created a train wreck in my head. Such thinking is never constructive and yet I am curious here, too, and wondering how it might feel. I want only to test the waters, am no more sincere than that, a clinical experiment I assure myself as I take two steps closer and tell Gloria I love her. She is sleeping, of course, and can't hear.

~

THE GARDEN IN FRONT of Matt's house has bluebeard shrubs, oleander, and Carolina allspice Cara has planted. The fragrance as I remember fills the area sweetly. Matt and I are having drinks this afternoon, and I imagine him spending his day first running sprints with the boys, as he told me at dinner, then coming home to write, perhaps later sitting out front reading *The Heart Is Strange* by John Berryman before finding his keys and driving downtown.

I arrive a few minutes early and grab a table for us outside at Bachman's. When Matt shows up, he takes the chair across from me, which puts his back to the sun. Voting on the Zell concluded this morning and for this I have a new strategy in mind, the turn of the screw as it will begin now, I suspect, if all continues to go according to plan. I wait until we have our drinks before raising my glass and issuing congratulations. "You're in," I say. "You have your slot. I can't give you an exact date yet." I explain our need to extend the invitations to the other authors and confirm who is available when and work from there. "But we want you, Matt, for sure."

I let him thank me, discuss the terms of the commitment, the lecture he will be expected to give beyond his reading. "Maybe on Bishop." I suggest then say, "Congratulations again, Matt. This is a huge coup and well-deserved. You've worked hard for this and I am certain the other committee members will love you once they have a chance to read your work."

Matt is in midcelebratory glee when my comment freezes his face like one of those old polaroid shots where the subject is captured forever in a half-executed smile, his eyes squinting and head tipped in surprise. "They haven't read me?"

"Not yet. But they will. This shouldn't bother you."

"But how did I get selected then?"

The question is rhetorical and I don't bother to reply. "The Zell is significant," I say. "The name will stay with you now. It's all about getting your foot in the door and taking advantage of the opportunity." As I tell him this, I see an additional measure of uncertainty cross Matt's face. I sip my drink then say, "It's all good. You're good. I've read you and can vouch for your candidacy."

He thanks me again, less assuredly this time. "I just assumed," he says.

"It doesn't matter." I have him now, I'm sure, this fragile poet, his ego righteous and ambition untilled. "So they haven't read you.

So what if they don't know you and are giving you a slot as a favor to me? You can still show everyone what a great writer you are when you have your reading. Don't worry about what people think."

"People already think something?"

"I mean when word gets out and those who didn't land a spot are bitter. It's nothing," I say. "Let's just ignore those who think you're getting preferential treatment. The writers who miss out this year we'll keep on our list for next. Hopefully we'll still have funds. Your invitation is long overdue."

"Mine?"

"Of course. We need to bring in lesser-known writers. It shouldn't concern you in the least that the others on the panel are unfamiliar with your work."

Matt rubs at his wrist. An honest fellow, a weakness, he feels compelled to say, "And yet it does concern me."

"Don't let it. No one will hold it against you. Not long term."

"All the same," Matt in reply.

I have him now and finish with, "It is all the same. Everyone takes what they can get. It's how the game is played. Opportunity is about leverage, not integrity. You owe it to your work."

"Even so."

"What now? You can't decline." I give him the word to use, place it there in front of him as I fully expect him to pick up and offer back to me.

"I'm afraid I have to. Decline, that is." He does this in a way that makes him appear almost relieved. How innocent he is, this scruff mop of a man who still believes in uprightness, who loves his wife so, his pure bent poems that aim to champion love with all the subtlety of a pudgy baritone standing center stage. How easily this went and how much it is sure to piss Cara off.

I feign disappointment and groan, "What's that? Matt, wait." I say that I went to a lot of trouble, which is true, covering my bases just in case, and ask him to reconsider. "Let me get the others to read your work and give an honest vote without pressure from me." I use the words *honest* and *pressure* here, say that we can slot him for late winter or spring, give everyone time, but we have to announce the full list soon.

"Maybe next year," Matt says. "I do appreciate this, though. I'd just prefer to go through normal channels."

"These are normal channels," I say. "Everyone we choose has an insider's endorsement to get things started. Look at past recipients," I list here all the most famous writers: George Saunders, Aimee Bender, Colm Tóibín, and Roxane Gay.

Matt seems to physically shrink as I present the list. "All of them are deserving and well-read. They don't need internal endorsements," he says.

"Nonsense," I reply. "Everyone needs a little help from their friends."

"I understand," he tells me. "I just think, in this circumstance, people expect more from a Zell recipient."

"So give it to them. Surprise them." I bring my sunglasses down my nose and say, "People love a good surprise."

"Maybe next year," he repeats.

I finish my drink. It's early in the evening and I'm already motioning our waiter for another. Before coming downtown I considered the possibility of raising Matt's hopes about the Zell only to inform him that his talents did not meet our standards, and how disappointed would Cara be? The risk in this was creating empathy over the loss of the Zell and pushing Cara and Matt even closer together. Ultimately, I decide to try something else, suspecting as I did that Matt was always fearful and reticent about the Zell, and having gotten the response I want now, I redirect our conversation, I am good at this, at moving seamlessly, serpentine in my narrative.

I suggest Matt speak with Cara if he's actually going to decline, and he tells me, "Cara will understand."

"Well, you know her best." I slide my glasses back up and adjust my chair. "I envy you, Matt," I say next. "Relationships are tricky, but you and Cara seem solid. Unconditional support is hard to come by. How many years have you been together?"

"Twenty."

"That's inspiring," I continue this way. "Marriage isn't easy and don't I know it. After a while relationships are like trying to keep the shine on a rusty fence post. The challenge is in how to best apply the polish." I laugh at this then say, "Marriage is a gamble, Matt. You work hard at your relationship, don't you? You do what you can to make Cara happy. It's all about keeping things fresh, isn't it? That's the key, don't you think?"

Matt finds my statement an odd digression, though relieved to not have me contesting his decision to turn down the Zell, and he answers, "'Fresh'? Yes, I suppose."

"Of course it is." I clap my hands. "At our core, Matt, we're restless creatures, intolerant of the mundane, excited by what is new. A marriage needs to understand this or it will turn stale and crumble like an old cracker. Now I'm no expert," I say, "but there are things I've learned, and isn't it possible the trouble we get into when trying to keep a relationship fresh is that we insist on doing everything together when in reality, Matt, when you stop and think about it, we are actually doing our spouse a disservice when we fail to focus on ourselves?"

Matt is puzzled by my statement, considers for a moment before saying, "You lost me."

I start again and say, "When you first fell in love with Cara, you did so because she was new and exciting to you. This excitement is what triggers our interest, and from there infatuation turns to love. Doesn't it then make sense that to sustain a relationship we owe it to our significant others to remain uniquely ourselves, fresh and interesting? And how do we do that, Matt? Certainly not by clinging to the other person, but rather by continuing to develop our own individual identities. How are we supposed to build a relationship if we become dull and predictable and lose sight of what first attracted the other person to us?"

Matt questions my theory and suggests that I am starting from a false premise, that people don't lose sight of their personal identities when they marry. "Moreover," he says, "building a relationship creates its own excitement and identity."

"Sure it does," I say, "for a time, but to what end? Most relationships are lazy, Matt. They cause us to surrender a part of ourselves to appease the other. It's no longer about personal identity and more about avoiding conflict. This is where things go south. We compromise our spirit, surrender ourselves without even realizing at first, and then we wonder why our spouse no longer finds us interesting. As a couple," I say, "we become absorbed into one and stop thinking in terms of who we are. Everything becomes *us* and *we* and this is suffocating. It's individuality that keeps a relationship fresh. Our personal self is the most important thing we can offer our partner. A relationship by definition means disparate entities coming together, so what sort of relationship is it if one or both of the parties stops being who they are?"

Again Matt doubts my claim. "A relationship means coming together, yes, and working together and being together."

"Sure, sure," I reply. "But there's more to you than being one half of a couple. You had a history before you fell in love with Cara and why should that stop now? There's something to be said for continuing to create a personal journey outside of a marriage in order to keep the relationship fresh."

Much as at dinner, Matt has now become uncomfortable with my claims, and, feeling a need to defend against all such suggestions, he tells me, "That doesn't sound right."

"Why?"

"Because it's adversative and narcissistic."

"Because I favor openness and freedom?"

"Because you place the self above all else."

"But that's just it, Matt," I avow, "I don't. I'm telling you that a fully realized self, that a liberated self, is best suited to create a lasting relationship."

Matt isn't convinced, responds with the obvious, "And you're a living example of that?"

"I'm a clumsy stooge whose current state proves nothing."

"Then how am I supposed to accept what you're saying?"

"By listening," I answer. "What good is any relationship if it doesn't liberate us? What good is it if we're unable to live our lives as our individual selves? I'm talking about all forms of liberal engagement, Matt. A truly bountiful relationship puts no restrictions on a partner." I wave both my hands in an animated gesture, remove all pretense from our discussion as I go, "Traditional relationships are untenable. The cookie-cutter definition and expectation placed on marriages in general creates tension."

I take another sip from my drink, measure my words carefully as I want to make my point without chasing Matt away. "The American notion, which defines love through our sexual fidelity, is stagnating, Matt. It's unnecessary and provincial. Love should not be about suppressing our physical lives to one partner. The prospect is soul crushing. We are bigger than that. We are better than that. If I love someone, that love must extend beyond our sex, otherwise it won't survive."

Matt still isn't buying and asks why sex should be centermost in establishing our individuality.

"Why indeed," I reply. "That's not up to me. It's just the way things are. Why have we as a society made sex so taboo? What are we so afraid of? Why does real freedom terrify us so? Why are we so staid in our relationships, so provincial in our lives? Don't you get bored sometimes, Matt? I mean honestly." The tables outside of Bachman's are black iron with thin rods for legs and palm leaf designs for feet. We have an umbrella in the center of our table and it's open now. My margarita has beads of condensation on the outside. Two women sit at the table directly next to ours. I don't know if they have overheard anything I've said, though they do glance our way.

Matt moves his chair further from the sun. He folds his hands lightly in front of him, considers his reply, and then says with instruction, as if I may have somehow failed to consider, "Has it occurred to you true love inspires intimacy and monogamy, and all discussion of extracurricular needs is a smokescreen for problems that already exist in the relationship?"

To this I answer, "That's a lot of hooey, Matthew. That's you being judgmental."

"I'm not being judgmental at all. You're free to do whatever you want, as long as you don't impose on others."

I lower my sunglasses again and say to Matt, "Not to worry."

Matt shoos a fly, finishes his drink, pauses again, then says, "I don't mean to sound like a prude, but I don't think the issue is about being puritanical, it's about a different sort of desire." He quotes Auden to me, speaks of his affection for Cara as: *The years shall run like rabbits / For in my arms I hold / The Flower of the Ages / And the first love of the world.*

"That's beautiful," I give him this. "But you're overthinking everything, Matt. What I'm proposing is that the human spirit is capable of tremendous generosity and a little individual time away from the marriage can be good for the relationship long term. To suggest two people cannot love one another deeply and profoundly while having sex with others is a narrow view."

"I don't think it's narrow," Matt remains unpersuaded. "I think people want to be in love and want to be monogamous, but we're clumsy and impatient and this leads to our looking for fulfillment elsewhere."

"Hell, Matt." I lean forward in my chair, pull my sunglasses off completely, and say, "I'm not concerned with fulfillment, I'm talking about getting laid. Don't you ever want something new now and again, if for no other reason than to refresh yourself and be reminded that life is large?"

Matt lifts his empty glass. The bend in his arm has muscle. When he looks my way he appears irritated and no longer willing to debate. He thanks me once more for the Zell then says of the rest, "The way I see it, boredom is one thing and love another. One we choose while the other comes and goes. I can't tell you how to deal with either, but for me my desire is my desire, if that makes sense. It's not a complicated concept, really, how I choose to love."

CHAPTER NINE

RETURNING HOME, I FIND Gloria in the front room watching the news. She has made herself a salad and poured a glass of wine. I drop my keys in the bowl, kick off my shoes, and sit in the chair as Gloria mutes the TV. She asks about Matt and I tell her, "He turned me down."

"What?"

"He said no."

"To the Zell?"

"To the Zell."

"Get out."

"No lie."

"But why?"

"Who knows? He's a poet. He claims he's not comfortable with my helping him."

"He said that?"

"Yep." I sink lower in the chair as Gloria asks for more details. When I tell her about the vote and how I explained to Matt that I was the only one to have read his work and had to persuade the others to give him the slot, Gloria realizes what I have done and scolds me for going back on my word. "You said you wouldn't fuck with them."

"How have I fucked them? I got him the Zell. He turned it down."

"Sure he did. You wanted him to in order to piss Cara off."

I stretch my legs and don't bother to deny it. Gloria goes into the kitchen and pours more wine, comes back and sits again in the chair. Her glass is filled too high and she nearly spills some before sipping. I watch her hand, which is steady around the neck. She has her hair pulled back now and to the side. I try and ignore how handsome she is. I am bothered when Gloria continues to complain about Matt and says, "You need to reconsider what you're doing."

I defend myself with gibberish and say that my activities to date are romantic in spirit, that I am a searcher of truth and looking to explore the bone-dense challenges of love. Gloria summarizes my claim with her favorite one-word review. "Bullshit." She says what I'm doing is brutal. "You want to hurt them."

"That's not true. I don't want to hurt anyone."

"Then stop."

"But I'm not doing anything," I lie. "I just thought if I shook things up a bit the truth would be easier to see."

"What truth?" Gloria answers before I can. "You want to prove all relationships are fragile? Well guess what," she raises her wine and says, "all relationships are fragile."

Rather than concede the point I change the subject, I am not interested in arguing or discussing Matt further, so I ask, "How was your day? I was thinking about you. I missed you."

There is a moment before she replies, before she is able to gather herself and snap back at me, where what she wants to do and nearly does is take the remote from the television and hurl it at my head. I am sure of this, I can see it in her eyes just before she groans loudly and tells me, "Do not go there."

I act surprised and say, "Go where?"

"McCanus."

"I didn't mean anything by it."

"Of course you didn't."

"Well, which is it?" I insist she can't be upset if she knows I didn't mean it. This causes Gloria to groan louder than before. She puts her glass of wine down on the table between our two chairs and says, "I didn't miss you."

I start to say that's too bad, I am playing a bit with fire and obviously that's how I like it, this back and forth and emotional poking of the dog. I begin to joke and sing a line from John Waite's "Missing You" when Gloria stops me and goes, "I heard what you said when you came back from New York."

"You heard me?"

"Say you loved me."

"Hell."

"You thought I was asleep."

"I did," I admit, "otherwise I wouldn't have said it."

"I'm sure."

"Yeah, well." I don't know what else to do now, I am not sure how to recover, though I try and go, "I was tired. It was a long day. I wanted to remind myself of the feeling but it wasn't real."

"Of course not," Gloria says again.

I tell her just the same, "I don't love you."

Gloria repeats as much to me then gets up, moves past me, reaches back for her wine, which she holds for a moment in front of her face and drinks. I watch her walk away from me and up the stairs. It's early still, too soon for bed I think. Gloria is already beneath the sheet when I come in. I strip and get in beside her, I can't decide if I should say more, unsure what I would say if I could say anything about loving her or not loving her, so I don't say a word as Gloria stirs and reaches for my hand.

Mostly when we have sex she is lively, robust and earthy, well-focused on how she feels, and I am happy when she enjoys herself. As partners in that moment, we are a feral and mutual force. In our sex she will push against me, wrestle into me before going somewhere else, somewhere all her own and where I can only try and give chase. Tonight, I hope she will stay with me, and I am glad when she moves toward me, takes the lead, kisses and lets me kiss her and touch her until she's ready, and then she straddles and rides on top.

She remains quiet, much more so than usual. I lay her back down, kiss her neck and shoulders and ears until she shivers and lets me think she came. She clings to me afterward, briefly and unexpectedly, still not saying a word. I am good now, I am finished and content, though I hold her as well, for whatever reason. Gloria is the first to roll off and onto her side where she exhales softly, the sound filled with confession I think, and while it's possible I may have gotten the sound all wrong, I move closer just the same.

CARA IS HOME WATCHING the news when Matt returns. She has made herself a salad for dinner and is drinking wine. He tosses his keys into the bowl, drops into the chair beside her, kicks off his shoes as she mutes the sound and asks how things went.

"Good," he says, then tells her about the Zell.

She isn't quite sure she heard correctly; she can imagine him saying he got the Zell or did not get the Zell, but, "What do you mean you turned it down?"

He explains how his nomination circumvented normal procedure and that, "I shouldn't have been given a slot."

"But they offered?"

"Technically. McCanus twisted arms. They hadn't even read my work."

"And so you turned them down?"

"I said under the circumstances I wouldn't feel right accepting."

"Wouldn't feel…?"

"Right."

There is a moment before she replies, before she is able to gather herself and construct a proper response, where what she wants to do and nearly does is take the remote from the television and hurl it at his head. What she wants to say, which is different from what she eventually will say, is that he's a fool and his decision has nothing to do with protocol but rather that he's a scared little rabbit and refuses to take his own work seriously, that it shouldn't matter how the Zell came to him but only that he has the opportunity, and Goddamn it why does he have to turn everything into a moral apocalypse? Why can't he just accept that Eric agreed to help because he could, that this is the way the world works and everyone else understands this?

Instead, she switches the TV off and sets the remote on the side table. "All right," she says. "What now?"

"Now? Nothing," he answers and, sensing her dismay and that his reply is all wrong, he adds, "It's okay. I'm good."

Of course you are, she wants again to shout, is angered by how easily contented he is and quick to be *good*. She goes into the kitchen and pours herself more wine, holds the glass by the neck, and says, "I think you should have taken it."

"But I couldn't," he defends himself this way, ignoring the holes in his claim, his self-righteous lip flap and high-road imperatives. He describes what was said over drinks, how McCanus made sure to let him know he was responsible for the invitation, how the rules were bent and people were bound to question his appointment. "Under the circumstances it would not have been right to accept," he says again then adds, "I think McCanus was relieved by my decision."

Cara returns to the front room, has her wine, her bare feet spread on the wood, her arches sore, she shifts left to right. "I don't believe that," she tells him. "Why would Eric bother to get you the Zell if he didn't want you to accept?"

"I don't know. It was an odd conversation."

"So now you're blaming Eric?" She's annoyed, tired, and hungry still after having only had a salad, and is quick to reply, "If you don't want the Zell just say so, but don't blame Eric for your decision."

"I'm not blaming." He nearly raises his voice and says, *You don't get it,* but is concerned how she might respond and doesn't want to escalate things further. "I'm just saying," he hates to think Cara is angry or disappointed and tells her, "we really only spoke about the Zell for a moment and spent most of our time discussing relationships."

She knows what he's doing, what he always does, how his main interest is keeping the peace and that's okay, mostly, but there are times when arguing a bit would not be a bad thing, when their solidarity becomes itself a burden, and what she really wants is to scratch and claw like two cats locked in a basket, screeching and brawling before lying exhausted together in sweet recovery. There is something to be said for this, too, she senses as much and blames herself for not letting go more than she does, for holding back, and for what now? The same peace and contentment she is ready to excoriate him for.

"Relationships?" she repeats the word as if it's a puzzle. "What about them?"

Relieved to change the subject, he presents McCanus's theory on love and marriage. He tries to be fair, avoids painting him with a red brush, though he does tell her what was said about the value in maintaining our individual selves and how most marriages would benefit from adopting a liberal view toward sex and allowing a revolving door of partners.

Cara puts their argument on hold here, again unsure she has heard right, and, looking at Matt, suddenly flush behind her third glass of wine, she raises her chin and replies, "He said what now?"

CHAPTER TEN

THE FIRST TRUCK ARRIVES towing a yellow crawler dozer to dig up the yard. I am upstairs writing. Fred barks and goes out back. Cara comes a few minutes later. Before the dozer begins to excavate, the sod is rolled away, put aside, and saved for future use. I continue my own work, glancing every now and again out the window. Fred returns to check on me, to be sure I am aware of what is happening. I rub his head to let him know all is as it should be.

~

I GO OUT BACK around noon. The yellow dozer is operated by one of the college boys. Cara works along the slope, creates impressions where six large stones will be placed and serve as steps down to the lowered part of the yard. I have moved my car out to the curb in front, while in the driveway an additional truck delivers trees and bushes and gravel. Cara has on a pair of brown gloves, which she removes as I approach. There is dirt from her work in the lines of her cheeks. I have brought her a water. We talk about the garden first and then as we walk toward the shade Cara mentions the Zell and apologizes for Matt's decision, says she regrets the trouble I went to.

"Not to worry," I answer appropriately. "It was worth a shot. I was glad to do it."

"You don't have to say that." She delivers the sentiment cold, apologizes again and lets me know, "I should have said something earlier. The first time you brought up the Zell, I should have warned you Matt might say no."

"You couldn't have known." I remain deflecting, though hope she might say more.

"But that's just it." She starts talking about Matt's tendency for reticence, his habit of shying away from events involving his writing. The pattern is well-established, Matt's happiness simple and ambitions small. "It's frustrating," she catches herself here and stops. I use the opportunity to say I find Matt wanting to earn his way commendable and am certain the others on the committee will love his work. I blame myself for not getting the committee to read Matt sooner and wish that I had explained all to Matt more clearly.

Cara won't let me take responsibility and says almost fiercely, "This is not your fault. This is not on you." She touches my elbow then draws her hand back, looks at me for several seconds before insisting once more the blame belongs on Matt.

I think how opportunity is a matter of chance and ambition brought together, and I am this close to agreeing with Cara and taking the situation somewhere new, but I remember what I promised Gloria and stop. This is supposed to be the end. If I need proof that what I saw at the market was but a flash glimpse of a marriage and no more representational of a full relationship than any other quick peek might reveal, if I want to somehow be convinced that love is layered and can be built up with foundation posts or torn down by any variation of high winds and rains, then the incident from our dinner and now with the Zell should be enough.

It should, yes, though the problem is I'm writing a book and need to know for purposes of closure what happens next; at what point does the bow bend and where does it break?

There beneath the shade of the one tree set to remain, my elm in bloom, I say to Cara that she should not be too hard on Matt, that he has created wonderful poems and if his character is otherwise lacking, if his personality does not allow him to take his work and champion it openly to new and awaiting audiences, if he prefers the shy existence of a poet who produces great verse and leaves it like a birdsong on the wind, if he entrusts the selling of his books to his publisher and marketing people, this should not be construed as weakness. "Not all men are cut out for testing their convictions beyond the comfort of their own walls." I submit this and watch as the cords of muscle in Cara's neck tighten.

I leave her there while saying that I have an appointment. Fred and I take a quick walk around the block and together we head off to Colossal.

~

GLORIA CALLS AS I'M halfway to the studio. I'm scheduled to work with a singer/songwriter named Michelle Joy and have to phone her now and apologize, promise to make things up to her tomorrow. Michelle is with Glassnote. I've listened to her songs and dig her sound though Gloria is better. I was actually thinking about this, about Gloria and her music, when my cell rang. A minute later I am making a U-turn on Parkwood and driving back home. Cara and her crew are still in the yard when I pull up. I park at the curb in front of my house and hurry inside.

Gloria's duffel is by the door. She is standing across the room pulling a few books from my shelf. I stop on the other side of the room, still processing what she told me on the phone, how she was moving out and thanks for everything. "Help yourself," I say about the books, I am clumsy and upset and don't want her to leave, though this I won't tell her. Last night after Gloria sighed and I rolled back toward her, we remained that way, holding one another, unexpectedly and curiously until I began to feel calm and dozed. Gloria was the one to get up first. It was early evening. She showered and dressed, said she was playing a set at The Veldrux later, and would I like to come? Had she asked me while we were both still in bed I would have said yes. Removed from her, I made an excuse, said I already had plans. "Break a leg," I told her. Staring at her now, I think of all the other ways I could have replied.

Gloria reaches down and pets Fred. I move another half-step forward and say, "If I had known earlier I could have helped you pack."

"That's sweet."

"Are you okay?" I ask.

"Me? I'm great."

"And this, then?"

"This is exciting, isn't it?"

"Is it? Maybe. I don't know. Why now?"

Gloria glances back at me as if I've asked something stupid. "It's not about now, Mac."

"Sure it is. It's always about now."

Removing a copy of Eckhart Tolle's seminal work from my shelf, Gloria tells me not to go getting all philosophical on her. "We both knew I wasn't going to stay forever."

"That doesn't explain why today."

"Today is just when things happened."

"Yes but what happened?" I want to know. "Is this about last night? Or before? About what I said? About Matt and Cara?"

Gloria resumes picking books from the shelf. It's unclear when exactly I made up my mind, though now that Gloria's leaving I am more inclined than ever to say that I really do love her. "Are you mad at me?" I ask.

"Why would I be mad?"

"About Matt and Cara."

"No."

"Then we're good?"

"I'm good." Gloria takes the books she has gathered—the two of mine, a paperback of Vonnegut and the collected works of Anne Sexton—and puts them inside her duffel. She looks, as always, inscrutable and with no sign of anger or injury of any kind. Still she doesn't explain anything more, leaves me to assume from her silence that I'm supposed to already know what's going on. I start over with a different sort of question, I ask about her new address. "You have a place?"

"I have a place."

"And money?"

"I have a place and money."

"And you're not mad at me about anything?"

"What did I say?"

"This isn't about anything, then?"

"It's not about you, Mac."

"All right." For whatever reason I can't quite accept and continue with, "So when did you decide?"

"I didn't decide," Gloria answers. "The opportunity came along."

"Just like that?"

"Just like that."

"And where are you going?"

"East Town."

"How did you find the place?"

"I have a friend."

"And this friend called you today?"

"That's right."

"And you're leaving me to live with him?"

"Don't be like that, Mac."

"But you don't want to live with me anymore?"

"Seriously," Gloria cautions, "let's not, okay?"

"Let's not what?"

"Make this into something it isn't."

"What is it, then?"

"It's nothing. I'm not leaving you because we aren't together. This isn't a breakup. We aren't a couple. I'm leaving because it's time. This is your house and I need to find a place of my own."

"But you're moving in with someone else. How is that any different?" I want there to be something specific, a point of contention in order for me to argue Gloria back into staying, though I think maybe the only reason I want her to stay is because she is about to go. When Lidia said as much to me that night I went by her place, I denied the claim about her as well, and now I wonder, given all the ins and outs, how am I ever supposed to know the truth about what I'm feeling?

I step back, sit on the arm of the chair, and, hoping for a favorable response, something to keep her here longer until I can figure out what to do, I confess about last night, tell her that I drove out to The Veldrux after all, that I caught her set and she was magnificent. I say this, "You were magnificent."

Instead of being pleased, Gloria walks out of the room and retrieves her guitar, comes back, and puts the case beside her duffel. I have no idea why what I said should upset her and ask, "What's wrong?"

Gloria is taller than Lidia, not as Nordic as Cara, more nimble and lithely limbed. I wonder if she is about to howl at me and criticize how secretive I can be at times, to point at the flaws in my nature, the way I make things difficult on purpose, that I couldn't merely accept her invitation and come to the club with her last night but had to turn it into a clandestine encounter where I arrived under cloak, slipped in and out after her set, hoarded my impression of her playing in order to leverage it now as I think serves me best. Despite how harsh this sounds, it is actually what I would like her to do, to yell and scream so I might apologize and say that she is right, no doubt she is, and that I do not blame her at all for being upset, that obviously she expects more from me and this is certainly something we can work on together if she stays.

I am good at this, at responding constructively to some harsh redress, which draws into question my ability to provide whatever it is I'm being accused of lacking. I'm always happy to confess my sins if such gets me what I want. Hopeful here, I'm foolish enough to think things are about to sort themselves out as Gloria walks toward me, leans close, and kisses my cheek. I reach for her, irrational in my confidence, but she is slippery as a conger eel, she escapes my grasp, gathers her guitar and duffel, goes out the front door, heads to her car, and disappears.

~

THE THREE BOYS IN Cara's crew finish up for the day. Cara comes from the yard last, knocks on my door, says she'd like to leave the crawler in my drive. I tell her no problem. I'm still reeling from Gloria's departure and my face must show as much as Cara remains on the porch and asks if anything is wrong. I say it's nothing and invite her inside for a beer.

Cara insists on removing her boots; she bends over in such a way as to allow the front of her T-shirt to billow. She shows the day's work in the rose tan of her cheeks. After starting the garden, having had lunch and dinner together, and now the incident with the Zell, Cara appears almost comfortable with me, familiar in a way she is still in the process of defining. I see her move a strand of hair behind her ear, the dirt on her neck and wrist charming somehow. She asks if she can use the powder room. She says this, not the bathroom or restroom. When she reappears, she has washed her face and hands. As if there is some necessity, being alone with me now in the house, she refers to Gloria, "I met your girlfriend earlier. She's very nice."

An innocent enough comment, I might leave it there, share none of what just happened with Gloria and move our conversation on to something else. Instead, I choose not to, for reasons I suspect were already formed when I invited Cara inside, a muscle instinct, my mind now in a perpetual state of plotting, I offer up a summary of Gloria's exit and admit that, "I didn't expect to feel gutted this way." I say that I was caught by surprise, though am quick to make clear that as Gloria was never officially my girlfriend and we weren't really a couple, our parting was more or less expected. "The less," I say, "being today."

Cara gives me a tender smile. She has large teeth and wide lips made moist by her beer. We are sitting at the pantry table in the kitchen now. Through the window I can see the yard at the start of its upturned state. With the grass and dirt and stones tossed about, everything appears in chaos. Cara says she's sorry to hear about Gloria. I tell her that I am, too, and, "Whoever knows, right? In terms of what I want, I mean, I always feel a step behind. Lidia leaves and I say, 'Oh yeah, that's what I want.' Gloria leaves and I say, 'Oh yeah, I want her, too.'"

Cara moves her shoulders and head in a sympathetic bob, suggests for Gloria, "If you want her back you need to let her know."

"But she does know and I think that's why she left. I think she knew before she left that I wanted her to stick around and that's what caused her to go. It's complicated," I say. "Gloria isn't one for commitments. She has her own idea of how people come together." I say this and wonder if Matt has said anything about my own views to Cara, so I go ahead and add, "Not that she was alone in fostering the ambiguity of our arrangement. I guess you could say I'm also something of a nontraditionalist."

Cara confides that Matt did mention.

"So you know." Despite my promise to Gloria—as Gloria isn't here—as much as I suspect Gloria's leaving was instigated by my treatment of Matt and Cara as much as by my whispering "I love you" into the dark, I am starting to calculate further the benefit to our conversation and say to Cara, "The truth is I may have given Matt the wrong impression. It isn't that I don't believe in love, it's that I'm clumsy and can't quite make my theories work when I need them to." I talk a bit more about Gloria, about what happened when I came home from New York, and how hard it is for me to get a real handle on my emotions. I pause just long enough for Cara to take in what I've said then confess, "It's a slog for me, for sure. The sustainability of any relationship, I mean. I'm good in the moment but the moments don't ever string together for long. I wish they would but I somehow don't know how to make this happen."

The sentiment causes Cara to react as I hoped she might, her features giving in to emotions of their own. I look at her, present myself as woefully frustrated and sad, so much so that Cara can't help herself, kind as she is and susceptible now, with her disappointment in Matt and the Zell brought to the surface, her transference of affection almost impossible to avoid as she extends her hand across the table, finds my fingers and squeezes.

Oh I am an ass, but how easy is this? Too easy, in fact. I allow my hand to linger just long enough inside hers, my eyes on Cara's as I slowly pull my hand back. The intent here is to let her know the moment has been registered by me. Whether she fully meant to or not doesn't quite matter, the point being that I am regarded as the cautious and prudent one. To act otherwise, with rash expediency, would only undermine any long-term agenda. Better to have Cara make the next move than to throw myself on her now in a moment of weakness. In this way the responsibility is hers.

I smile softly, or at least I think what I am showing is a tender smile. Cara is of firm Norwegian stock and governs her emotions with strict discipline. Reaching for my hand has been a breach and I have played this well. I stand with my beer, go to the window, and look for Fred. Cara takes a few seconds then mentions the trees and brush to be planted by the end of the week. She leaves shortly after this, her beer on the table. I turn and say as she is walking off, "See you tomorrow."

CHAPTER ELEVEN

MATT PHONES AT NOON and asks if we can get together and talk. He sounds troubled, a woebegone weariness as if he hasn't slept for some time. I, too, had a troubled night. After Cara left, I wandered through the emptiness of my house, searching for remnants of things that were not to be found. I called Gloria but she didn't answer. I called Lidia and got the same. I called my lover—not that one but the new one—though hearing her voice made me feel worse than before and so I told her I was travelling and made a date to see her next week. I went for a drink, went for a drive, went to Colossal for a time, and then back home where I got in bed only to find the space around me too wide. An ocean of room with Gloria gone. I thought about Cara then Lidia and Gloria again. I called out, "Hello?" just to hear a voice. Fred appeared in the dark and I stared long enough to make out the wag of his tail.

This morning, I wrote a fresh scene for my novel. I have no idea where the book is going now but the scenes have a density to them, an emotional tick, like the undercurrent of a great swell, and from this at least I am wise enough to let the momentum pull me along. I write of Matt sitting up in the early evening, waiting for Cara as she is late tonight. He has fed the kids, has fixed a macaroni casserole, which he keeps warm for her; careful with the heat, he protects what he has made with a tinfoil covering and sets the temperature to what he thinks is safe. When she comes home, he is reviewing the poem he's working on, the narrator describing a trip taken years ago to England with a lover who has since vanished completely from his life. *The old Ankerwyche Yew / there by the Thames / two thousand years old / where kings courted queens in the grass grown and gone. / He has seen up close / again and again / seen in pictures / recognizes the earth and sky / the branches as they reach / like hands / muddy strewn / with fronds of spiny needles / at play forever.*

He asks if she is hungry and she says she wants to shower first. He returns to the kitchen. Outside there are young children playing. She comes down and asks about Eli and Lia and he tells her they have come and gone. Somehow the phrase upsets her and she says, "You should have told them to wait and have dinner with me."

"I texted you," he says. "You were not forgotten."

"Even so," she grumbles still. She knows she is being unreasonable, but can't quite stop.

He serves her casserole on a white plate, puts the plate down on the table while asking once more, "Are you hungry?"

Afterward they watch TV, first Netflix and then the news. In conversation she speaks as if distracted, sips her wine slowly. At ten she goes to bed. He stays downstairs, turns the TV off, and sits for a time in the dark where he thinks about her distance, her displeasure with him even as he admitted yesterday his judgment was off, that he never should have turned down the Zell and would see if he couldn't still get the slot. He expected this to please her, but she became even more incensed and accused him of playing two sides against the middle, of getting what he wanted and then paying lip service to her concerns. "Honestly." She said nothing more, went outside and worked a hoe into their garden soil before returning to watch *House of Cards*.

It's close to midnight by the time he heads to bed. The moon has set itself outside their window, a white sliver of ice, and he follows the ray across the floor, finds his wife, and slides in beside her, silent enough for now, and warms his feet.

~

CARA IS OUT IN the yard but I have not spoken with her today. I wonder if she said anything to Matt about last night, I wonder if this is why Matt is calling, though somehow I suspect not. I'm working with Michelle at Colossal this afternoon, and when Matt calls I suggest we meet at Fendunckle's at five. Fred is waiting downstairs and I take him with me to the studio. I do not stop out back and speak with Cara first, but head straight to my car.

Michelle is already at Colossal when I arrive. I apologize again for yesterday, I say that I've given her songs a good deal of thought and have several suggestions. The best of Michelle's material is a tune titled "Bury Me Whole." We record the piece with an altered chorus and a piano placed beneath the lines of her guitar. Our effort is definitely an improvement and Michelle is pleased when we finish. I suggest we sleep on the cut and talk tomorrow. Cara texts just as I am getting ready to go meet Matt. She says she didn't realize I had left, asks if we can talk. *Possibly later,* I type back.

Matt is waiting outside as Fred and I arrive. We find a table on the patio and I loop Fred's leash beneath the leg of my chair. I have forgotten to eat lunch, and, starved, I order a Reuben. We chat briefly about Colossal and Michelle before Matt tells me why he called. Distressed, he confides about the error he made, his prideful decision concerning the Zell and that he is wishing now for a do-over. "If there is any chance," he asks, and I, too, give him a sad look and say no, the invitations went out last evening and everyone accepted. "I see," he says. "It's just that," and here he presents his situation with Cara.

How mad she is and how worried this makes him. Such a concern, he can't really say how things got to this point, but here they are and what a mess he's made and while the issue isn't new, the subject of his reticent ambition, there seems something different and more toxic in her complaint this time.

I let him talk, listen as he speaks of Cara's attitude toward him now and how she regards his contentment as a weakness. He has ordered McDowell's rum on the rocks. I'm not familiar with McDowell's and never drink rum straight. I sip at my own drink and wait for Matt to continue. He rubs his neck, pushes his sunglasses up, and tells me, "Being a poet there's little to wish for beyond the writing. I thought for a time I might teach at a university, and when my poems began to publish I did apply for a few positions. Maybe I should have accepted the offers. Cara wanted me to. She was willing to move. I was offered a position at Pepperdine and Cara could have worked year-round in the California sun. Instead I liked the high school and decided to stay."

"There is certainly nothing wrong with that." I have every intention of defending Matt here, I am quite capable of playing two sides against the middle and, having come this far, am fully invested in seeing things through to the end. Matt reaches down and pets Fred; he appreciates my support and insists he was naïve not taking the Zell, that he should have realized the decision would upset Cara, that her regard for his lack of ambition was a stew steeping all these years, and now the issue with the Zell has tipped the pot. He wrings his hands, sips more rum, and says, "She sees this as a pattern, my unwillingness to do more."

"You write," I say. "Isn't that enough?"

"Apparently not. Cara thinks my turning down the Zell is about avoidance."

"What is it you're avoiding, exactly? Fame and fortune? These women," I defend Matt this way, "what is it they want from us? You do good work and you're an honorable man. Why can't Cara let you be who you are?" Our food arrives and I dig in ravenously. Fred sits up and I give him a piece of meat. Matt has ordered a turkey club, though he doesn't seem hungry and picks at the insides. I keep us on point, concentrate on Matt's dispute with Cara, and say, "If your being content to write your poems and share them as you do is a problem, if this has been brewing between you two before and the Zell brought the issue to a head, well, I am sorry for that Matt, but Cara's out of line and you have my full support."

Matt again thanks me, though being Matt he says, "She isn't entirely wrong. Maybe if I moved outside my comfort zone better things would happen."

"Jesus," I have him now, I can't help it, everything continues to be so easy and here I go. "Listen to you. Why should anyone aspire to be less content? You're happy for fuck's sake. Isn't contentment what we all are chasing? Good Christ, what I wouldn't give for a moment of what you have, to be content and create great work and not forever be chasing my tail. If Cara can't appreciate what a unique man you are, if this is now a serious dispute, what can you do?"

"I thought if I could still do the Zell."

"That's impossible, Matt. And why should you do it when you don't want to?"

"But I do want to," Matt says this as if I might still help though I've already told him that ship has sailed.

"What you want," I say, "is for Cara to understand, but she doesn't. Obviously this is an issue and I do feel bad for having offered the Zell to you, for my part in all of this, but I must say, Matt, Cara's position isn't fair to you." I present him with a countering example and say, "No one is telling Cara to move on from SunGreen after all these years and work on larger projects. She's content and why then can't she let you be, too?"

Matt is clearly uncomfortable, he is trying to cover for Cara, wanting everything to be as smooth as a freshly laundered sheet.

He starts to say again how things are complicated and that truly he and Cara want the same thing, but I stop him, insist that none of what he's saying suggests Cara wants what he wants, that the situation is unfortunate yet clear now. "Isn't it? Listen, Matt, I'm no expert and you know this, but from my perspective, for me, Matt, you need to take your position on this seriously. You're obviously happy with your life and if your wife isn't receptive, if after all these years you're finding out she isn't satisfied and is dismissive of your contentment, well I don't blame you for being pissed."

Fred scoots closer to Matt who still hasn't eaten much of his sandwich. Matt sighs and tries to address what I've just said. "I'm not the one who's mad," he tells me. "I don't want to be mad. If all it takes is my doing the Zell to make Cara happy—"

"Goddamn it Matt, forget the Zell," I cut him off. "Why should you have to do what makes you miserable just to please Cara?"

"Because she's my wife."

"And how is that fair? Look," I say, "I get you want to make her happy. I understand the theory of necessary adjustments and all, but you can't be changing what's fundamentally you to please someone else. That's crazy. It's a slow death to you and your relationship."

"And yet," Matt insists, "I want to do it."

"Suddenly now?"

"That's right." He reaches for his drink, sad in a way that nearly moves me, and, thinking there is something I might still do to add a further wrinkle to the game in play, I tap the table three times with my middle finger and say, "If that's really what you want, Matt, if you're so concerned with Cara, I have an idea. I have something that just might help."

~

CARA AND HER CREW are gone by the time I get home. The excavating of the yard is finished and half the hill is complete. The bi-level slope is taking shape, the stone steps down, and borders where the crushed rock path will be laid out. I survey the yard then go inside with Fred, find the two books of Matt's poetry I purchased, and begin leafing through. My idea is simple, my intent a little more complicated. Now that Cara and Matt have begun to bicker, I'm curious to see how hard I need to hit the wedge in order for the wood to split. If Cara remains at the heart of Matt's concerns, if he fears his position on the Zell has caused her to detach from him in ways he can't endure, how will he fix things? How indeed. Fix for sure. And what will Cara think then? How confident and completely full of shit I am when I tell Matt I can help.

I sit with his poetry, read until I find just the right poem. Given Matt's knack for writing visually lyrical rhythms, a sort of Meg Myers meets Townes Van Zandt keen wound howling, I'm sure I will come up with something. The beat of Matt's writing, his material hovering between hope and longing, affection and despair, makes his poetry prime for song. I anticipate having to restructure his work a bit, loop around and repeat select lines to create a chorus, identify the hook within the meat of Matt's prose, though essentially the lyrics will be his. The process should be easy once I find the right poem. From there I will call Gloria. Three birds with one stone. There are possibilities within the possibilities and I consider all.

After an hour, I narrow the prospects down to two pieces. I call Gloria but her phone goes right to voicemail. I wonder if she is playing tonight. I have not heard from her since she moved out. In the time she's been gone I've thought of her more than I like. It has occurred to me that this is what she wants, that her leaving makes the absence in my heart grow fonder. Whether or not I am right about this or merely imagining Gloria's strategy, I can't be sure. I want to believe she still cares for me and, clever as she is, knows missing her challenges my fortress walls.

I leave a message on her phone then turn my attention back to Matt's poems, review the work I've selected, and get to crafting them into lyrical form. My favorite begins: *I am pitched / in the mooring of your morning after / the shape of things / in the bedsheet draw / without you now / offering what is to come. / I am left / In the sun / day's paper left / in the toss of stories spread out / in the soft light fading / on my floor. / I wait for your return.*

I type out the piece in total and send it to Gloria in a text.

~

THE NEXT MORNING, CARA comes while I am writing and rings the bell. As a rule I do not respond to this sort of interruption, but hearing Cara's truck pull into the drive, having not called her back last night, I'm curious to know what's on her mind. Hitting save on my computer, I come downstairs.

Before Cara arrived, I had just written a scene in which the Cara in my novel is "on hands and knees, casting rows carved and dug in the earth, alstroemeria, aster and catmint, ruby star and mango punch. She knows how to coax them, to work the dirt as if in prayer. She supplicates and teases. Through the spring she plants, through the summer she tends, sets back the leaves and brush in the fall, lays out plans in the winter, prepares herself for the chill season when all things refuse to flower, though it is in the same dark earth that the cycle began not so long before." I think of this as I open the door.

Cara is dressed more or less as always, in work shirt and shorts, brown boots laced, her hair pulled back away from her face. Something, however, is different. I've not seen her with makeup ever during her workdays, but here her eyes are lined just enough to accent the green and give her gaze a fullness. I step back and invite her inside. She stands on the porch and removes her boots. I am about to say she doesn't have to but catch myself and let her take them off.

Her socks are white against the tan of her calf. We go into the front room and sit in the two chairs. I apologize for not getting back to her after we texted and had said we could possibly talk later, "But then the day got away from me."

"You were with Matt," she says.

"I was for a bit," I reply. "He called about the Zell."

"I know."

"He truly regrets."

"Yes. I'm aware."

"It's hard on him," I set our conversation this way and confide, "Your disappointment has him worried, not that he doesn't deserve you being pissed. We spoke about this. I understand your side. It's unfortunate Matt can't do more with his work, but people are who they are." I am trying to construct just the right tone, mindful of my delivery, and I do not yet mention anything about hoping to use one of Matt's poems in a song, leave that little secret for now as I say, "Matt has a narrower view than you. He gets overwhelmed and can only handle so much. He's a hell of a writer. I like him, but I get why you're mad. It's understandable. It's frustrating."

Cara doesn't reply to this but says instead, "I just want to let you know I won't be working on your garden after today. Everything here is under control. You're in good hands."

"You're leaving me?" I respond this way and with some surprise.

Cara tells me it's for the best, that she has other projects that need her attention. I protest and say if she is more comfortable leaving I understand, but that I was expecting her to finish what we started. Again my statement is meant to draw her out and here she repeats, "You'll be fine."

I press for more and ask, "Is this because of what happened in the kitchen?"

Cara can't quite control her expression even as she answers, "Nothing happened in the kitchen."

"And yet here you are." I look at her and go, "I like your eyes."

"Stop."

"You're wearing shadow."

"I didn't come to talk about this."

"Yes, you did."

She starts to get up but I raise my hands and say, "Okay," and ask her, "Tell me what you came to talk about, then."

"I already have. I want you to know I won't be around after today. If you have any questions—"

"Can I call you?"

"About the yard."

"All right." I accept her decision and leave things there while bringing us back around to Matt. Cara doesn't want to talk about Matt anymore however and says, "We are fine."

"You and Matt? Good. I'm glad to hear." I wait just long enough, allow Cara the chance to leave if she chooses. When she doesn't, I go for broke and say, "I did however see the way you looked at dinner when Matt went on too long about love as the glory prize. I know what you were thinking. It's harder than that, isn't it?"

"Just stop."

"All the best intentions and still we're human. How long can we desire one thing before effort and disappointment wear us down and all the adjustments we make become tantamount to putting grease on stripped gears?"

"I'm not going to listen to this."

"Then go."

"I love Matt."

"I'm sure you do. He's your husband and for how long now? Twenty years. I don't see how you do it. I mean, love, yes. But the things that happen over twenty years, the way things change and how steadfast you are. It's commendable." The word sounds cold and isn't lost on Cara.

I sigh tellingly and speak again of Matt. "I know you're frustrated with him and wondering where all of what's happening now will lead."

"It's not going to lead anywhere."

"But it has to, doesn't it? I mean something's going to happen one way or the other."

"You're wrong," she tells me.

"Am I? About what?"

"Everything. All of this."

"What this?"

"I know what you're doing." She is sitting quite still in the chair, barely moving at all.

I wait for her to say more, but instead she remains silent, she appears to be waiting for me. I don't disappoint; I go ahead and remind her of our discussion at lunch, how I understand and respect her commitment, her defense of marriage as a grand experience, though for me, from the outside now, the whole thing looks like a tug on the water drawing flatbed loads down the shore by sheer endurance. This is my interpretation of marriage for Cara, and to this I add, "I know it's all about going the distance and committing to necessary adjustments, but what if the adjusting winds up as more sacrifice than intended? What if we wake up one day and realize the adjustments we made weren't done for love at all? What if we were simply looking for a rapprochement to sustain what we have even when what we have is no longer what we want? What if our relationship has become a convenience, if we're carrying on out of stubbornness because we'd rather stay than risk leaving? What if we're so determined to love that we forget what love is?"

Cara insults me here, says that I am just looking to cause trouble. She is right, of course, but I don't say this, not exactly, though I do ask, "What about desire? What about accepting that after twenty years things change?"

Cara does get up now, though I stop her from leaving by speaking about the trajectory of love, the passion that burns at first like a rage, consumptive in its heat, and how, in time, the blaze requires more tinder and brittle sticks to keep even the slightest heat coming from the flame. "Here we are in middle age," I say, "in the patch of time that passes so quickly we barely notice when the itch arrives and in a fury of unanticipated doubt, the reckoning begins. What we want then is our release, to feel again as we once did, and we wonder when that chance arrives if we are brave enough to take it, to know with a pulsating certainty we should, and wait to see what will happen next." This is what I'm curious about and say to Cara, "This is what you're feeling now."

I consider speaking again of Matt's deficiencies, addressing Cara's strengths, and how what once worked well for them was bent beyond repair. I could say all this and more but it seems nothing else is required, and so I skip the rest and come from my chair, lean in toward Cara, and kiss her deeply.

In the affairs I've had, in these first moments, I nearly always find the eagerness of surrender comes as a relief. Whatever gamesmanship came before has ended and allows for willing participation, a collapse into warm waters, which no longer terrifies but is entered readily and eagerly. There is nothing different this time. Together we enter, curl and embrace, take ourselves up the stairs, into the bedroom where, fully immersed, rejecting all pause or reflection, we fall into bed, peel away our clothes, and become the measure of our want in the way hunger takes hold and overwhelms all else.

Afterward we say nothing. This is not surprising. There is for now nothing to be said. I wait until Cara gets up and dresses before getting out of bed myself. By the time I have showered and returned to work, Cara is out in the yard. I see her from my window, a shovel in her hand, standing on the edge, digging down in the soil in order to create impressions to set the stone.

CHAPTER TWELVE

HOW STRANGE, BUT AS he's lifting weights this morning, repping what has always been a manageable heft, pushing through a series of eight, the burn that comes is suddenly filled with the most peculiar pain inside his chest, not so much a hot flash bolt but bleak and hollow as a wind through tightly closed shutters. On his back he struggles to complete the set.

~

GLORIA CALLS AS I'M feeding Fred. It's already after three and I've just finished writing. I usually don't write so late, but sleeping with Cara has inspired me and I have no trouble transitioning back to work. This is not callous, it's what I do. My writing is an exploration of the story unfolding, and finally now I have the narrative taking shape. I don't sensationalize our sex but examine it for what it was, and is. I look to identify the consequence and anticipate the collateral damage. That I am the root of the damage is irrelevant in terms of my story and by that I mean the one I'm writing.

Gloria sounds good. "You sound good," I say and too soon go, "I miss you."

To this she replies that she may have left a shoe in the closet and when I get a chance she'd like me to check. I tell her that she should come have a look for herself. Gloria ignores this and asks about the text I sent. I explain how the verse is from Matt, that since turning down the Zell he's become desperate to make things right with Cara. "I'm thinking," I say, "if we can present some of Matt's poems to a new audience through song this might work."

The idea sounds phantasmic when I say it out loud and yet I go ahead and ask Gloria to help. I've not considered rescinding my offer to Matt even after sleeping with Cara; I am actually more intrigued than ever to see what comes of things now, and as the situation is set up to bring me close again to Gloria, I ask her once more to, "Say yes. I know you write your own lyrics, but this is a unique opportunity that could work for everyone." I tell her if she can come up with a tune using Matt's poem that I promise to take the piece along with some of her other originals and pass them on to people I know in the business.

Gloria doesn't answer right away. I picture her on the other end, sitting with her legs folded in some large cushioned chair no longer mine, or maybe in bed with her new lover. I see her and wait for her reply. I am sure she's thinking to ask what it is I'm actually up to, or how I never managed to get any of my contacts to bite on her music before. Instead, she finally goes, "Sure, Eric. I'll come up with something and give you a call."

I thank her at once and start to say maybe we can meet and discuss, go to Colossal and work up the tune together, but before I can get the words out Gloria has already said goodbye and clicked off the line.

~

LATE THAT AFTERNOON, MATT waits for Cara to come home, first inside preparing their dinner and then out on the porch. He is on the porch as she pulls into the drive with her window down. Seeing him, she rolls the window up. The forecast for this evening is rain. The forecast starts with clouds.

The distance between the driveway and porch is only a matter of twenty feet, and yet walking toward him seems to take forever. She attempts to smile, attempts to steady her gait. The dirt from the day has gotten under her nails. She goes inside, stands at the sink, and scrubs. He heats the oven and removes the fish he's prepared from the fridge. The kids come and go. Soon they will be back at school and the house will be quiet. "You're quiet," he says as the fish cooks. She has poured herself a glass of wine and taken it outside. He comes and sits on the steps beside her and asks about her day.

She tells him that she is moving on from Eric's garden and will leave her crew to finish. One of their neighbors passes and they wave. Sitting there, what she finds peculiar, what strikes her as most strange, is how even after this morning everything is the same. She thinks about this, of how she has no intention of telling Matt what happened, no plan to let her sleeping with McCanus do damage to her marriage in any further way. What happened is just that. An incaution. A once-in-a-lifetime mistake. But how can she dismiss it as nothing when her every thought now is filled with what she did?

She gets up and moves across the front walk, between the bushes she has planted. Matt remains on the steps. She stands atop his shadow, recalls what Eric said about being steadfast in her marriage and how it may seem commendable but is actually something else. *What if you wake up one day and realize the adjustments you made weren't done for love at all? What if you've simply been stubborn and so attached to the idea of love that you've actually forgotten what love is all about?*

Matt goes inside and checks on dinner. He has cooked the fish in butter. He prefers beef but tonight he will eat as she does. The glass pan is set between them on a hot pad in the center of the table. He serves her first. She samples what is presented without comment. For a minute or more they are silent, the only sound coming from their silverware and the drape across the window moved by the breeze. She hasn't showered before dinner, wishes now she had and wishes to wash herself and can't quite understand why she didn't.

He thinks to tell her about the plan to turn one of his poems into a song but wants to save the surprise until there is actually something to hear. Since quarreling over the Zell he's hesitant to promise anything; he doesn't want to say too much too soon. "So," he says and tells her just the same.

She lifts her head slowly. What she hears first is "Eric and I" and nothing else. As the rest registers, as he describes the prospect of a song, she looks at him and laughs. The sound she makes begins low, like the rumbling of some powerful pressure working its way through clay and loam until it breaks the surface of the earth and expands loudly through the air. Her eyes are in a squint against her cheeks, lifted and swollen, made red as her mouth opens wide and he thinks that she is happy, ecstatic even, and so he joins her, laughs as well, believes what a joyous moment they are having until through her laughter she curses and begins to shout.

Instantly she wishes she could stop herself and take everything back. She wants to start over, to do nothing more than acknowledge his news with a nod and say how nice and let it go at that. Instead she reacts to the mention of McCanus with a floodgate rush. Once released she can't recover, while caught unprepared, he stares at her, tries to make sense of her reaction, which cuts at him like a jagged crush of ore.

She has her hands down beside her plate, lays them flat and wants to keep them there, to steady herself as the echo of her laugh remains. He waits for her to explain and she does so viciously, says it's wrong after turning down the Zell to take advantage of McCanus again, that this idea of creating a song from a poem is a gimmick at best and whatever was he thinking and why can't he just leave Eric be? "Stay away from him, stay away from him, stay away from him!" She is slapping the tabletop now, about to burst into tears, all of this so unlike her, and startled he can only wait until she pauses long enough to breathe in order to ask what's going on.

Such a mystery. Such an exchange. She apologizes quickly enough, does not so much explain as say the matter with the Zell has left her worn and she doesn't think it's a good idea to trouble Eric anymore. "Let's not do this again, all right?" She says this softly, no longer reproachful, though he takes it as such just the same.

After dinner she goes upstairs to shower. He cleans up the kitchen, waits for her, busies himself with matters of no significance, then heads up to find her but she is already in bed. She has a copy of McCanus's second novel with her. Hearing him on the stairs, she turns out the light.

He stands late by the window. All is quiet. She sleeps. In the stillness he thinks of time, of what has passed and what remains. He thinks of how he feels, and how he feels what he feels, of the energy it takes now for what used to come naturally. That nothing is as before he understands. Everything is cumulative, each decision causing some incremental matter of change. In the morning he gets up when she does and fixes her coffee as she dresses for work. When she comes down, he tries to engage her in a pleasant way, doesn't dwell on last night, wants all to be as it was before, only she doesn't care to talk. His voice disturbs her and she tells him, "Hush."

Harsh, yes, she knows this, she realizes she is losing control and fast, right? What is she doing? Before leaving, she comes and gives him a hug. The embrace is more conciliatory than affectionate, though he accepts it just the same.

He finds his shorts and running shoes and heads to the high school where he joins the boys in their sprints and in the weight room. He is both collegial and deferential with them, aware that this is their time, their turf, and he doesn't look to interfere or defeat them. This morning, however, his mood is such that he gives them no comfort, no encouragement, nothing but his head down as they get ready, his back to them as they cross the line.

He jogs home, showers, then takes a pad and pen and sits out on the porch for a change and writes. Without his laptop, seeing the sampling of his own hand drafting his words makes him even more intimately aware. He thinks about last night, as he came up the stairs and saw the glow from their bedroom extinguished before he reached the landing. He whispered for her and waited for her to answer, writes of this now, his words drawn through the letters of his own hand causing him to feel exposed as he composes: *I call / her name / ask if she's okay. / Are you? / She tells me / sleeping. / Says she is.*

CHAPTER THIRTEEN

THIS MORNING, WHEN CARA rings the bell, I don't answer. At this point I'm thinking we need to establish some rules of engagement and how we're going to proceed from here. I'm already tired, having gone out last night—restless and hoping I might run into Gloria, I drove downtown. The rain had started and I parked inside the structure on Fourth then jogged across the street to The Grotto for a drink. I was thinking about going to Caber Hills and seeing if Lidia was there, though I really didn't want to confuse myself further so I finished my drink then headed back outside and drove to Colossal.

Frankie was there with Rose Grayne and two guitarists, Billy Sweet and Ricky Perl, whom I'd worked with before. Rose was with Verve, a great singer, jazz stylist, a Dinah Washington meets Jill Scott sort of serious talent with a CD about to drop, including three songs we worked on together. Sweet and Perl sat on the couch, each with their instruments held in their laps like natural extensions. I asked how everyone was doing and Frankie told me, "Rose got ripped off."

"Hard truth," Sweet piped in.

"Boyfriend troubles," Frank again.

"Always, right?" Perl added. "Uh-hum."

"Sorry to hear," I said.

"Is what it is, you know?" Rose heaved a sigh. "But thanks."

"Fucker stole her money," Frank said.

"Copied her signature on a check and cashed it to himself."

"Nine thousand."

"Shit."

"Gone like the wind, right?"

"The cash and the boyfriend."

"Did you tell the bank the check was forged?" I asked. "The bank is liable. They have to pay you back."

"Assuming Rose can prove it."

"He copied her hand," Sweet said. "Laid it right down so it's hard to tell."

"Bank's already skeptical."

"Black woman and all, you know?"

"Least ways they're going to make her prove she wasn't part of it or didn't actually sign."

I took all this in, I looked from Frank to Rick to Bill to Rose who sat with her head tipped back, the set of her jaw raised tight while her eyes flashed hurt in a way that made clear the money stolen wasn't the only thing on her mind. Rose's woe hit home, the comedy of every relationship, the macabre slapstick, which played out whenever two people attempted to come together. "The things people do," I said. "Stole your money and broke your heart."

"On and on." Sweet picked up the thread on his guitar, followed by Perl, and played us through until Rose began to sing and Frank set the mics so we could record.

Around ten, I called my lover and she met me at our motel. "Lucky for you," she said of her being able to get out, she told me next time she wanted to fuck at my house. I said we'd see, I knew I wouldn't let that happen, would instead bribe her with a better hotel. After we screwed, I told her about Cara, about Lidia and Gloria and everything that did and didn't connect the three. My lover laughed at all my news and how tortured I seemed to be. "Come here, lover," she said, "and tell me again."

I didn't get home until late and then Fred and I walked out back in the yard. The floodlight shined into the garden. Fred was happy to have me home, ran around, took a dump somewhere near the new cherry tree. I made a mental note of where the shit fell, told myself I would clean up the mess in the morning.

~

CARA TURNS TO KNOCKING next. Fred barks. The front door is unlocked after our morning walk but I don't expect Cara to try the handle.

She tries the handle, sticks her head inside, and calls my name.

"Working!" I shout down.

"Eric!" she yells back.

It is this already. I curse loud enough for her to hear, hit save on my computer, and come downstairs.

The makeup Cara wore yesterday is not there now. She walks toward me. I stand with hands on hips and let her approach. "I thought you were done here," I say.

Cara ignores my statement. Outside, the boys from SunGreen arrive to work the yard. Cara has parked at the curb, for a quick getaway, I suspect. She addresses me tersely. "What are you doing?" she wants to know.

I reply, "Writing, I told you."

"With Matt."

"What with Matt?"

"His poems. Your music. What is this?" she asks, louder this time.

I explain what she apparently already knows, that Matt and I discussed using one of his poems in a song and how, "This was after the Zell, before you and I got together."

"We're not together," Cara snaps back, and when I correct myself and say that isn't what I meant, she heaves up her shoulders and tells me to stay away from Matt. "You're not his friend. You can't work with him now."

Her demand rankles me, the insinuation that I am somehow singularly to blame for our sleeping together, and to this I say, "What about you?"

Cara stands two feet in front of me. In her work boots, in her cut-off bibbed overalls and green T-shirt beneath, she appears stern and impervious, fields my question and tosses it back. "We're not talking about me," she says.

"But shouldn't we? If I can no longer claim to be Matt's friend where does that leave you?"

"Where it leaves me is none of your concern."

"I never said I was concerned. I'm just asking."

"Well stop," she insists.

"All right." I consider saying goodbye and returning upstairs, but here is Cara in my house, in the center of my living room, barging in uninvited and disrupting my day. Her vehemence creates resistance and strikes me now as necessary to address. I fold my arms across my chest as if to demonstrate my resolve, and starting back in I say, "If you're worried about my saying something to Matt about what happened, you needn't. I'm well-practiced in this sort of thing and have no intention of saying a word. Matt asked for my help after the Zell, is all. He wanted to make you happy and who am I to say no? We thought doing something different with his poems might be a way to impress you. And, yes, I understand that my looking to help your husband while sleeping with his wife is a bit incongruous, but we all make up our own reality, isn't that right?"

"I don't even know what that means," Cara shouts. "What does that mean?"

"It means your truths and my truths and Matt's truths are not the same. Our realities and perceptions are different. People live in ignorance every day. People live with lies, both told and concealed, all the time." I confess to not being a good friend, and that I've slept with other men's wives before, though I do not do so to hurt anyone but simply because I can. I enjoy distorting other people's realities, I am inclined for sport to carry out a bit of harmless manipulation, and tell Cara then of how I carried on at a recent barbecue with members of my university department, that I purposely pitted three graduate students against one another with a fabricated claim of having Martin Amis to dinner and an invitation I planned on extending to one of the students. The whole of the evening was a carnival show as the three fawned and vied for opportunities to impress me. Eventually the night ended with the two male students in a near brawl while the female student used that moment to pitch me in the privacy of an upstairs bathroom. Such incidents are innocuous enough, though with Cara now the penalties are more long-lasting, I understand.

"I'm not oblivious." I tell her this as I must, without apologizing for anything, and explain how it is not my way to feel bad about the things I've done, that I believe in the firmament of free will and that we act as we do because we choose to, and why feel bad then when we make decisions? I answer my own question, I tell her that free will does not suggest sound judgement, that being free means we are unimpeded for the most part in our actions but those actions aren't guaranteed to be sound, and as we are equipped with reflection and the capacity to evaluate our conduct through hindsight, it is essential that we not lose track of this ability. "I feel bad for Matt," I say, "but that's all, and honestly even that I wish I didn't feel."

For her part, Cara doesn't want to hear about me. "I'm his wife." She says this in a way that is at once ridiculous and gloomy. She repeats her demand, does not want me working with Matt, as if this rather than our sex is the most sordid thing she can imagine. I consider her mandate misguided and say that I have no intention of quitting on Matt now, that what's done is done and as for the rest, "Matt is excited about doing the song. He believes it will make you happy. Maybe the possibility is no longer valid, but he doesn't know that and I think preserving his happiness for a little while longer is not such a bad thing."

Cara is standing much as before, hands on hips, her head in an endless pivot, as if dodging the words I am sending her way, and she hollers, "It doesn't matter what you think. I told Matt last night."

"You told him what?"

"The same thing I'm telling you."

"You told him you didn't want us working together?"

"After everything, after the Zell."

"After everything?"

"You know what I mean."

"But I don't. Did you tell him about us?"

"No, of course not."

"And still you said you didn't want him working with me?"

"I don't want you near him."

"And he didn't find that strange?"

"Why should he?"

"He's not suspicious?"

"There's no reason for him to be."

"Well," I shouldn't but can't keep myself from saying, "there is a reason. He just doesn't know."

Outside, we hear the sound of a truck as the gazebo arrives and Cara's crew begins to unpack and transport the sections into the yard. Cara goes to the window in my kitchen. I do not follow her. When she returns her mood is unchanged and doubling down she says to me, "I don't like you much. And not just because of what happened. I don't trust you."

"I never suggested you should."

"You shouldn't have to. People should be able trust one another."

"And when I kissed you?" I ask. "Did you trust me then? You could have stopped any time. I have no power over you."

Cara considers this then replies, "Whatever I did find attractive about you was a mistake. You're not Matt."

She says this and I answer at once, "Isn't that the point?" to which she curses me and says that I'm an ass. Turning from me, she starts back to the door, tells me that she has said all she came to, that she expects me to do as she's asked and stay away from Matt, and when the garden is finished I can pay my bill and not see her again and that will be the end of it.

As ever, I can't resist, because I am who I am and remain determined to know exactly how things will end, assuming this isn't the end just yet; because of this, I do not acquiesce and let things go, don't allow Cara to walk away, but am curious still, as I have a narrative to construct and no way to do this without asking Cara, "Then you don't want to talk about us? You don't want to explain why you slept with me?" I call after her, I am thinking of where things started, of what I saw the first day I spotted Matt and Cara at the market, and where things are now. Whatever my sleeping with Cara proves, whatever this confirms about Gloria's claim that all relationships are vulnerable to being fucked with, I need to know more and go ahead and repeat my question. "Why did you sleep with me? You owe me this much," I say purposely, knowing this will piss Cara off, and it does.

She stops and pivots. Cara is a strong woman. I enjoyed that with her, feeling her strength, the muscle to her as she has worked for all these years wrestling stump and root in and out of the ground. I see this power now as her shoulders push back and her neck tenses as she shouts loud enough that the boys in the yard might hear, "I owe you?"

"It would be nice to know." I remain composed, have no reason to bark, and say simply that she knows why I wanted to sleep with her: because I'm an ass, because I believe in the potency of free love. "In theory," I say, though I have never made this work for me because my heart is a confusion, I tell her that I am confused as I thought to still love Lidia and now I think that I may love Gloria. "And yet here I am sleeping with you, though obviously we aren't in love so why did you do it?"

Cara takes the heels of her hands and presses them against the side of her head, she makes a face as if she is actually in pain. I am certain she has thought of little else since we fucked, has asked herself the same, wondering why, and can't quite allow herself to answer. Here, however, she replies to me in a way I don't expect. She doesn't launch into a mournful confession and say it was because she lost her way, or that she has loved Matt so long and with such blind conviction that she actually forgot what passion felt like. She does not say she was confused and realizes now more clearly than ever that I am not Matt, or that the things I argued about love and our individual needs, what we can offer and what we can keep, appealed to her in the moment but that moment is gone. She doesn't say any of this but calms her head with a more immediate claim, lowers her arms until she is so totally still I think for just a second she has forgotten me. It is here that she replies as I could not have expected from her, and tells me, "Because I wanted to."

It is enough. We go upstairs after this and fuck like the feral dogs we are.

CHAPTER FOURTEEN

I SHOWER AFTER CARA leaves. The boys outside are installing the gazebo. Fred is with them. Cara is gone. The repeat performance of our sex lingers in the house now. I go back to my desk, open a window despite running the air, and, inspired again, as I can't help, I write about Cara coming home last night and Matt telling her of our plan to use one of his poems for a song. What a scene it makes with Cara howling and Matt dumbfounded.

I check the time, give Fred a quick walk, then grab my keys and head off to see if I can catch Gloria at the diner before her shift ends. I have no idea if she is working today, no idea if she's quit the diner and taken another job, no idea if she's read Matt's poem, or why I can't stop thinking about her nearly a week after she left me.

Danny's is a popular west side diner serving hippie hash omelets, brioche French toast, Cajun catfish, and Danny's famous cheddar-stuffed burgers. The ten tables and counter space are set inside a rectangular brick building, the sign on the roof flashing *Danny's* in orange neon lights. Gloria is there, working with one other waitress on the floor. She wears a gray Danny's T-shirt and jeans. It is the end of lunch and I take a table near the back window.

Gloria comes over and says, "Hello, my name is Gloria and I'll be your server." She doesn't look surprised to see me, asks what she can get me.

I order a chicken salad sandwich toasted, "Hold the chicken."

She smiles. The diner is busy even at this off hour. I watch Gloria as she walks away. Seeing her overwhelms me and I begin to tear at the end of my paper napkin in order to have something to do with my hands. I remember once I was attending a conference in Delaware, a woman was on one of the panels with me, a midlist writer, quite handsome and intelligent. I was attracted to her right away. We sat side by side on our panel and fielded questions from the audience, our subject "Deconstructing Social Consciousness in the Modern Novel." I listened to her answers and took note of how comfortable she was— not the least bit affected or smug, each reply coming as if conversing with a friend. I immediately went and bought one of her books and stayed up late that night reading and was riveted by her prose, which was graceful and brilliant and touching without being sentimental. The story was about a medical student who volunteers at a clinic in Uganda and is followed overseas by a boyfriend she may or may not love. I went to bed that night dreaming wildly about the writer. For the next two days I behaved like a smitten schoolboy, following the woman, talking to her when I could gain the courage, attending her reading, and finally taking her to dinner where we had an enjoyable time and ended the night with a perfectly proper kiss. I was certain that I had fallen in love, but then I flew home the following day, got on with my life, and did not ever seriously think of her again.

That I think of Gloria still and have not forgotten her, even after she moved out, I assume means something. I have also not forgotten Lidia, and what does that mean? As skeptical as I am, as much proof as I have now that love is a jerry-rigged construct from which no couple is safe, the harder it is becoming for me to doubt it. Gloria picks up my order, brings me the burger and coke as she knows I want. I would like to talk with her about us, I hope to say something in support of our affair and why she should move back in with me. Before I can, however, Gloria takes her cellphone out of her back pocket, texts me, then walks away.

I click on what she's sent and find a link to the song she's composed for Matt's poem. Recorded on video from her phone camera, Gloria is sitting against a white wall, in a chair, in what I imagine must be her new digs. There is a ceiling fan overhead, the shadows flickering in a silent swirl. Gloria plays a picked-out third fret in E and G that catches me right away. When she starts to sing her voice is low and longing, moving up the register toward the chorus like a perfect wave. *I am pitched / in the mooring of your morning after / the shape of things / in the bedsheet draw / without you now / offering what is to come. / I am left / In the sun / day's paper left / in the toss of stories spread out / in the soft light fading / on my floor. / I wait for your return / want for you / for your return / hope you never know / that I am waiting not / waiting for your return.*

I play the song again while I eat, I am giddy with what I hear. It shames me to think how little I did for Gloria's music when we were living together. Her talent deserves better. The few times I did reach out on her behalf, I did not follow up, did not make a concerted push, and why was that? Hurriedly now I make two calls, one each to Daniel Glass at Glassnote and Laurence Bell at Domino Records. I get through to both and tell them I'm about to send a link their way and they should listen, as a favor they will thank me for. Ten minutes later, Laurence and Daniel both call me back.

I finish my lunch, wait for Gloria's shift to end, then go outside with her and sit in my car. She tells me she can't stay, that she is meeting someone. "Five minutes," I say, and she checks the time.

I keep things professional, thank her for the link, tell her the song she's come up with is amazing. "Truly," I say and explain how both Glassnote and Domino want to hear more. "They're offering development money for us to cut additional songs," I say. "I've worked with Dan and Laurence a bunch. Either company will be a solid fit."

Gloria takes the news in stride and refuses to give me too much, even though I can tell she's pleased. In sending me the link it's apparent she also knows the song is good and that she and Matt are a nice fit. I discuss a plan for cutting new music, including more Matt poems and Gloria originals. I say I will throw in Colossal time for free and she and Matt can split whatever cash Dan and Laurence provide, "Though we'll have to pay musicians and the development money won't be much. Still, assuming either Dan or Laurence like what else we present," I say, "they'll want to sign you. This is a career changer. I told them about Matt and they're intrigued. And they love you. I reminded them I sent songs of yours their way two months ago and they're going to listen to those as well."

I'm feeling confident. I touch Gloria's shoulder and she moves away. I would like to woo and charm her now, and am tempted to speak of love as if I might actually mean it, describe the empty nights since she's been gone as the hollowest of holes into which I've fallen, and I have fallen, I want to say, but Gloria is not one to woo this way, so I stop and ask instead, "How are you? Are you happy? Are you well?"

Gloria doesn't reply to any of this. If she is playing me for some further reaction I can't be sure. I wonder if I should tell her about Cara, confide how crazy things are and that she was right about everything and if she would only come back now I promise to mend my ways. I want to apologize and let Gloria know but doubt my saying as much will work in my favor, so I stick to business and tell her that she needs to come by Colossal and sign a management contract allowing me to negotiate for her. "You should meet Matt and we need to pick three more poems and go over your songs and start laying down tracks for review." I ask about her schedule.

Gloria says she can come by the studio tomorrow at four. She thanks me. Just like that, formally as if we weren't once lovers and I hadn't just done her a serious solid. She gets out of my car and heads to her own. I find my cell and call both Daniel and Laurence again. Twenty minutes later I have a development deal with Glassnote. I then call Matt and give him the good news.

~

LIDIA PHONES AS I am driving home. I'm not expecting this; I have just finished speaking with Matt when Lidia says she'd like to talk and can I come by the restaurant tonight?

As a reflex, not knowing what to think, delighted Lidia has contacted me, I ask if everything is all right. She assures me, "Yes, of course," as if the question is unnecessary, and says she'll see me around seven and clicks off the line.

Cara's crew has left for the day when I get home. I walk around back with Fred who immediately goes and christens the gazebo. Fred's a big boy, part lab and part pit, sweetest dog I've ever had but can piss a mountain stream; I'll have to train him off the gazebo and onto the trees. The garden is coming along, the new shrubs and brush planted, the remaining flowers and trees arriving soon followed by the gravel path and fountain. The setting is tranquil. I can't quite explain what I've done, but I do like the look of the yard. I take a picture and send it to Lidia, I imagine myself sitting out back with Gloria, and wonder what Cara is doing now. I spend an hour in the front room rereading Matt's poems, find three more I think will work for songs, type them out, and email them to Gloria. At a quarter to seven I drive to Caber Hills where Lidia is talking to diners, moving from table to table.

I go to the bar and wait for her there. On my way downtown I played Gloria's new music through the speakers in my car. Hearing her sing, I was convinced I loved her fully and deeply and lamented nothing more than her leaving. No sooner do I walk into Caber Hills, however, and see Lidia than I'm convinced I still love her as well. That I vacillate this way between the two puzzles me, and yet I know the issue is not my being torn between Lidia and Gloria, but that my attitude toward love is fickle and fleeting. A conundrum, this time I tell myself I will do better, though what I mean by this exactly I haven't a clue.

Lidia spots me and smiles. The whole of my heart aches for her alone now and my knees shake as I kiss her cheek. She says she is glad to see me and holds my arm as we walk up to her office. I'm pleased by this. Lidia closes the door after we step inside. She goes to the bookshelf and takes down a bottle of Woodford and two glasses. I sit in the chair. Lidia leans against the front of her desk. She has on a black skirt and white top. Her hair is neatly arranged for presenting herself in public, the Caber look I used to call it, her features given soft shading, her eyes hazel and lips mauve. Her office is a modern ergonomic design done in silver and glass like the restaurant below. She hands the whiskey to me and says, "Cheers."

We talk about the garden. Lidia thanks me for sending the picture and asks when it will be done, and can she come see?

"You want to see?"

"I do."

"Great. Come by any time." I bend forward and put my glass on the desk. Lidia is directly in front of me, she touches my shoulder as I lean close. This continued affection is peculiar, and, unsure of what's going on or why Lidia wanted to see me, I ask, "So, what's up?"

Lidia sips her drink and assures me again everything's fine. "What about you?"

For a moment I think to answer honestly and let her in on all that's happened with Cara and Matt and Cara again, with Gloria, too, as she has left me, and yet sharing all of this with Lidia when I don't yet know why she asked me to stop by seems ill-timed, so I simply say I'm good as well and I'm glad she called.

Lidia nods her head as if I've said something significant, and, touching my shoulder again, she says, "We're great friends, aren't we, Eric?" She pronounces this in such a way as to keep me from insinuating more. "After everything we've been through, we somehow managed to get out before hating one other, and on good terms, as I do feel close to you. It's good that I can still call you and you can call me. That's the most important thing, don't you think?" Lidia says.

I'm not sure how to respond other than to say, "Sure. Yes, of course."

"We have a history, we know one another completely, which is such an advantage for getting on."

"What's this about, Lid?" I'm becoming suspicious now, all the precursory chatter is unlike Lidia who is most often straight to the point. I wonder if she's met someone, after her sous chef, if she's called to tell me she's fallen in love.

Lidia continues. "We've survived the worst of us and still care for one another," she says. "Experience has taught us what works and what doesn't. We're lucky this way. We know now that we don't actually function well as man and wife, or as permanent lovers, but as friends we do, as friends who truly trust one another, without ulterior motives or designs. We want only what is best for each other," she says. "How many people can say that?"

"And so you've called to tell me what?"

"That I'm going to have a baby and I want you to be happy for me."

"Of course, I'll be…" *Wait.* "What?" I make Lidia repeat herself then ask, "What baby?"

"Mine, Eric."

"Are you pregnant?"

"No."

"Then...?"

"I almost told you the other night," she says, "but things weren't final and I decided not to."

"What do you mean final?"

"I've always wanted a child."

"I know. I know. So what is this? Are you adopting?"

Lidia explains that she has contracted a surrogate, that she has her eggs and a donor dad all set and ready to go.

This is too much information for me to digest, and I wave my hands and ask Lidia to, "Hold on. Wait now. What dad?"

"I have an anonymous donor."

"You went shopping?"

"I selected a father. I know his genetic makeup, his intelligence, and education all without having to deal with him personally."

"And this is what you want, to mix your eggs with some mercenary sperm popped into a surrogate baby-making blender?"

"That's cruel." Lidia cautions me not to take that tone and I know at once she's right. "We tried long enough," she says. "I want to do it this way now, for me."

I realize I have no right to object to Lidia's decision and that it's generous enough she is sharing her news with me. Even so, I can't help feeling sorry for myself, for the reality that Lidia is moving on completely now and has no need for me other than as a friend. I should be accepting, but can't quite get there and blurt out, "Why this way, though?"

"This way is best."

"No, it's not. Best would be if I was the dad. What about me?" The last thing on my mind when driving out to Caber Hills was the prospect of fathering a child, and yet when I make my offer to Lidia I'm entirely serious and hurt she didn't think of me before. That she wants to have a baby made from her eggs and some odd sputter dick's sperm is an insult. "Fuck me," I say, and mean this both as an offering and a condemnation.

Lidia sighs loudly and moves behind her desk as if our discussion is about to devolve from a friendly disclosure into something more formal. She runs through her list of reasons and lets me know that she is happy for our time together and very much wishes for us to remain close, but that's all. "Don't fight me on this." She says she's looking forward to her new life and raising a child, and to appease me, whether or not it's true, she adds, "Of course, I considered asking you. You're a brilliant man, Eric McCanus, you're handsome and funny and possess many of the qualities I need."

"But?"

"But you're also crazy as corn beef pudding, Eric. We would drive each other mad trying to raise a child. I don't want to do this with you anymore. We're divorced. This is my decision and my child."

Stung twice now, I ask if her surrogate has already had the insemination. Lidia tells me everything is scheduled, and when I start to argue further she makes it clear my effort is futile, so I stop and decide to take the high road. I stand in front of the desk, let Lidia know this is all swell news and I'm happy for her and am sure she will be a great mom and whatever she wants from me, I'm her man. We talk a bit more and then I say I have to go, and do so while turning around only once to look back at the office door, now closed.

~

I DRIVE TO FENDUNCKLE'S where I order three drinks in quick succession. Lidia's news has shaken me in ways I'm ill-prepared to handle, and, recoiling from the bombshell that my ex-wife, whom I may or may not still love, is planning to have a child without me, I decide to become sufficiently drunk. The bar is dark and loud and the whiskey goes straight to my head. Sozzled, I call Gloria. When she answers, I start in chattering right away and ask as if it's the most natural thing in the world, "What do you think about having my baby?"

Gloria hangs up.

I call her back and this time when answering she asks in turn, "Have your baby do what?" We laugh at this, and then Gloria becomes serious, addresses me more as she did this afternoon, and says it's important if we're going to work together that I promise to keep things strictly business. "No drunk calls. No talking about us."

"Fair enough." I don't tell her about Lidia, I don't want to complicate things more, and ask instead what she thinks of the new poems I sent. "They're great, aren't they?" I fill my voice with a level of enthusiasm meant to demonstrate that I am all about the project and over our baby talk.

Gloria says she is reviewing the poems now, and that she'd like to choose the musicians who play on the demo, as she wants to get her friends a few extra bucks. I ask who she has in mind and when she tells me I say sure. I invite Gloria to join me for a drink, to talk about the poems I say, but she doesn't bite, cautions me to drive safe, to go easy on the booze, and that she'll see me tomorrow.

~

CARA PHONES NOT TWO minutes later. I hold the phone hard against my ear and listen as she says she needs to see me. I tell her that's impossible. "Tonight's no good," I confide and mean this in more ways than one.

"It's important," she insists, and does not add please, not yet ready to plead though she is close. Despite myself, I can't help but feel for her. I recall a time when Lidia and I were on the outs and I had an affair with a woman named Marcela Stern. Marcela was a community outreach administrator with a husband and child of her own. Despite my making clear our affair was a casual thing, Marcela began calling me and asking when we might get together, professing her affection beyond all point of reason and turning desperate when I put her off. For a month or more I tried to maintain my distance, even as we were fucking, but slowly Marcela's persistence began to wear me down. Just as I was starting to wonder if I might have feelings for Marcela after all, I happened to spot her by chance on the street, walking down Harden Avenue, her coat misbuttoned and her hair wild. She carried a shopping bag under one arm and strode hurriedly like a toy soldier with no sway or jiggle in her hips. I realized at once how pity was not the same as affection, and after one final fuck during which I kept my boots on and was distracted by the smell of peppermint on Marcela's tongue, I quit the affair and came to terms with my divorce.

Cara says she's sorry for shouting at me this morning. She understands that I have sympathy for Matt and that this is one of the things she loves about me.

As I am drunk and suffering the effects still of Lidia's news and Gloria's continued distance, as my head is swimming in rye and I am pondering my next move on a dozen different fronts, it's hard for me not to burst out laughing at Cara, and it's equally hard not to snap back and howl that I don't have time for this and tell her that a fuck is a fuck is a fuck and should not be construed as anything more than that. Instead, I think of Gloria and Lidia and what a mess I've made of things, and, feeling sorry for myself, I announce back into the phone, above the ruckus of the bar, with a combination of empathy and enmity, cruelty mostly, though I pretend it's not, "I love you, too."

CHAPTER FIFTEEN

HUNGOVER, I WAKE IN the guest room again. It's late for me, after eight in the morning, and Fred is nudging my face. My head feels like the shattered remains of a crushed boulder, while even my breathing is too loud of a sound. I sit up and my equilibrium follows a few seconds later. I walk tentatively and let Fred outside. It takes several minutes more to get back upstairs and into the shower where I stand beneath the tap allowing the warmth of the spray to pass over me until I feel almost human.

Slowly, the pieces from last night come back to me. I remember Cara arriving at the bar. I remember our going out to her truck where we kissed and fondled one another in the parking lot like teens. It was a sloppy session that ended with Cara in tears, not from anything I did or said, or at least as I can recall. Caught up in the whole of our affair, she spoke of "us," and of Matt; she felt a need to decide what to do and looked to me for counsel. The irony was nearly too absurd to even consider. Just the same, I offered advice: I said there was no point in acting rashly now and confessing anything to Matt, that however hard it was to keep all of this a secret, it was best to say nothing and give ourselves time to figure things out. We went round and round a bit until Cara agreed and then we kissed some more before I returned to the bar and Cara drove off.

I let Fred back inside, dress, and go into my writing room and do what I can to work despite the gray pulse pounding in my head. I'm not much for coffee but drink what Gloria left behind. For the next several hours I struggle to compose a fresh scene, what I imagine about last night as Cara went home and what may or may not on its own be true. I picture Matt reading Auden when Cara pulls up. The light on the front porch is circled by two white moths. Lia and Eli are still out with friends. Matt watches Cara park her truck in the drive. She has stopped at the Gas 'N' Shop and washed her face in the bathroom, she is nervous, tenuously composed, afraid she will start shaking as she comes up the steps and onto the porch.

Earlier in the day she had texted him and let him know there was a tree she had to pick up, a drive she needed to make tonight, and that she would not be home till late. He offered to go with her, but she texted back that she was already gone.

He shopped for dinner, fixed a meal for himself and the kids, ate in front of the TV where he watched the news and tried to concentrate on what was being reported, but mostly his mind wandered. He thought of her and what was happening now, whatever it was, what he didn't understand even as he spent hours of his day writing about exactly this. Tired, his weariness troubling to a point where he grew angry, he thought, *Enough.* All this energy and effort to love and be happy and where had that brought them? Year after year to here, to discord and a disorder he can't explain. Something had changed; the dissonance between them that they'd always managed to tame had grown too loud. The mechanism they counted on was breaking down, and what if McCanus was right? What if the effort to love singularly and forever was unrealistic, impractical to wish for, and impossible to achieve?

He considered this, then immediately dismissed the idea. He had loved Cara forever, been in love, and this had not changed. He told himself, repeating it again and again and again like a Gregorian monk soothing himself until his faith was restored.

He greets her warmly now. She touches his shoulder as she passes, she doesn't stop but tells him that she has to pee. When he comes inside, she is in the shower. He waits on the bed. She steps from the bathroom already wrapped in a towel. Covering herself rather than walking naked around the room is a clear indication of her mood and he knows this. After twenty years he is more than aware of the signs, his motherboard tied to hers; even if he didn't want to notice, it would be impossible now. He talks for a bit and asks about her drive and picking up the tree. Her reply is vague. She gets him to change the subject by asking about his day then leaves him to dress. Downstairs, he goes back out on the porch, resumes reading Auden and *O Tell Me The Truth About Love: When I asked the man next door / Who looked as if he knew / His wife got very cross indeed / And said it wouldn't do.*

She comes down in the shorts and T-shirt she will sleep in. He asks if she had a chance to eat and she says yes. They go inside and sit and watch TV before she leaves again and heads to bed. He does not say anything to stop her. McCanus has sent him the link to the song Gloria came up with and he plays it again; he has listened several times already and is moved deeply. Impressed by Gloria's talent, he enjoys what she has done and is looking forward to tomorrow.

By the time he goes upstairs it's late. Lia and Eli come home and sleep soundly, dreaming as young people do. He envies them, he thinks of them in the morning when he rises and the house is quiet. At the high school he runs sprints against the boys. Back home he writes. Sometime after three he winds up his work and heads across town to Colossal, he leaves her a note but doesn't text or call. Driving east, he hums the melody to his new song, louder and louder as he gets farther from home.

~

I WRITE UNTIL TWO, then go downstairs and eat a sandwich. I think for a time about Lidia and imagine her baby and wonder what it will call me. Uncle Eric? How strange will that be? I think about Cara in nothing more than an exasperated way, and, finding Fred's leash, we take a walk. The day is warm and the fresh air helps remove the remaining haze of my hangover. By the time I leave for Colossal, my head is clear and I'm ready to make music.

I reach the studio after Gloria and Matt and find them talking together. Matt has brought copies of his books while Gloria has printed out the poems I sent her way. I have also printed out the poems I plan to use, having marked them up with suggestions for how I hear the prose being introduced as lyrics. Gloria sits beside Matt on the couch on the far side of the studio. She is playing her guitar as they talk. The other three musicians are setting up. Matt stands as I come over. Frankie is there checking the mics. I gather everyone together and explain that I'd like to start with Matt's poem-songs and record Gloria's originals later this week. I ask Gloria if she's come up with anything for the additional poems and she says she has a melody and lyrical framework "kinda sorta" roughed out.

We go over the new tunes with Gloria's ideas presented first. The musicians follow her lead and improvise before I offer suggestions. I work on the bridge and change the chorus and a few other things around; I do not alter Matt's words, but build a refrain from his prose as I did with "In The Mooring." It takes an hour before we have enough to try laying down a cut. Throughout the process Matt is more engaged than I would have expected. Not just a casual observer, not there merely to meet the band and stand off to the side, he offers suggestions as well, has his own ideas on the vocals and how he hears the poem sung in his head.

Gloria is receptive enough to test Matt's interpretations, she says "no" when she doesn't like and "yes, yes" when something works. They establish a quick rapport. By eight o'clock we've recorded two songs and roughed out the direction we want to go on a third. As the songs are entirely new, I want to sleep on them and revisit tomorrow. We send out for Chinese and decide to eat and then see if we can lay down a fresh cut for "In The Mooring." I ask Gloria how she's holding up and she says, "You know me, I can go all night."

The musicians have heard Gloria's original performance of "In The Mooring," and structurally there is little I want to change. I suggest an arrangement with very limited instrumentation, the drums using brushes, the keyboard and bass placed lightly behind the guitar. I take Matt into the engineering room as Gloria and the band record. Matt stands beside me and listens to Gloria, at one point surprising me as he grabs my arm and whispers, "She's wonderful," and smiles straight through for the rest of the song.

~

GLORIA CALLS MY CELL as I'm driving home from Colossal. "Coffee?" she invites me. We meet at the Clover where I ask why she didn't just suggest coffee before we left the studio, to which she says, "The studio's for business."

We sit in a booth, Gloria across from me. Our waitress is no longer young; she wears a pink and white uniform, a white cap, and white shoes. The uniform is humiliating and I smile charitably as she comes to our table. Gloria takes her coffee black. I've had too much coffee already today and order a Danish and water and wait to hear what Gloria wants to talk about. I am, as always, hopeful, imagining a scene where Gloria has changed her mind about having a baby with me, where she wishes to thank me properly for championing her music. I picture our reconciliation followed by a remarkable campaign where Gloria's musical talents are introduced to the world and put on full display. A tour is planned as her CD with Matt's poems and other originals goes gold, goes platinum, wins every conceivable year-end award. We will buy a new house together; will tour and travel the world; will become an inseparable and extremely successful and powerful couple; will be influential and generous as part of our success; will love one another fully and unconditionally; will raise our children—a girl and boy—to be creative and kind, appreciative and polite. We will grow old together in the sort of glorious harmony emblematic of our artistic efforts, and in the end, content, we will be grateful for our time as a couple and how lucky we were to have lived and loved one another.

This I can see, though Gloria has other plans; she has no interest in discussing the status of our relationship and wants rather to talk about Matt. "I like him," she tells me. "He's sharp. He's funny and shy, but not timid, and he has a great ear. His poems are seriously amazing, his understanding of wordplay and phrasing, his rhythms. I wasn't sure how things would go, but he actually gets what it takes to turn his words into song. I like working with him," she repeats. "He makes me think of Leonard Cohen and John Berryman."

"What do you know about Berryman?" I can't resist.

Gloria snaps at me, "Shut up. You think you're the only one who reads?" She quotes "Dream Song 29," inserting my name into the poem: "There sat down, once, a thing on [Eric's] heart / so heavy, if he had a hundred years / and more, and weeping, sleepless, in all them time / [Eric] could not make good." As soon as she finishes, she gives me a look which insists I tell her honestly, "What are you up to, McCanus? What's going on?"

"I don't know what you mean."

"Right. This, Eric," she flicks her hand back and forth between us and then up and out toward the window. "With Matt and these songs?"

Disappointed, I insist I'm up to nothing and swear that I'm trying to make amends, that since the Zell I felt bad and wanted to help Matt fix things with Cara.

"Bullshit."

"Bullshit?"

"Bullshit." Obviously Gloria doesn't believe me. "That's not what you're doing," she says.

"No? What am I doing then?"

"You're adding chapters to your book."

Ahh. "If that were true," I try to put the pressure of explaining back onto Gloria and ask, "why would I be offering to work with Matt now?"

"I don't know," Gloria admits. "That's why we're here. For you to tell me."

"But I have," I swear again, admitting that I was looking to mess with them before. "But all of that's over now. I got the answer I want. I know Cara and Matt are nothing like how I first saw them. I get it. Every couple's susceptible, isn't that what you said? Besides, I promised to stop fucking with them and I have."

"Have you?"

"I swear."

Gloria holds her stare until I'm forced to look down. "And what about Cara?" she asks.

"What about her?"

"Are you fucking her?"

I have always been drawn to Gloria's face, how handsome she is in that sort of Midwestern no-frills way. With some people, late in the day, as they tire and appear more vulnerable and worn, their features become less attractive, while with Gloria the opposite is true, the deepening of her eyes and no-nonsense turn of her lips adding to her attraction. I can't for the life of me remember what I've told her about Cara, all the conversations running together, the things I may have confessed and what Gloria already knows, but I don't believe I mentioned the latest and ask her here, "What makes you think that?"

Gloria puts both hands around her coffee mug and dares me to deny.

I argue back anyway and say, "Do you know how sexist you sound? Even if I wanted to fuck Cara, which I don't, what makes you think I can so easily make this happen? All women don't just want to fuck me."

"Smokescreen, Mac," Gloria rolls her eyes and goes, "When you resort to modesty as a defense I know you're lying."

I have no comeback for this. I am already wondering if I should confess about Cara and think this may be better in the long run, I am still debating when Gloria says, "It doesn't matter to me who you sleep with, McCanus, but you got me involved in this project. We're working with Matt now."

"Which would be a problem if I was actually sleeping with his wife."

I continue to deny it and watch to see if Gloria might believe, but she knows me too well, laughs and says, "McCanus, you are so full of shit." Before I can respond, she warns me again not to involve her in any of my nonsense. "It's bad enough messing with Cara and Matt on your own," she says, "but this is my career, my music, Glassnote is interested and honest to God, Eric, if all this blows up and Matt pulls his poems."

"That won't happen," I assure her. "Everything's good. Matt's on board. You saw how happy he was tonight."

"I did see. Which will make things even worse if he finds out."

"There's nothing to find out."

"You can't fuck with people, Mac, and think that's going to make you feel better about yourself."

I groan and insist, "But I feel fine about myself."

Gloria ignores me and says, "I don't want to see him get hurt. I like Matt, even if you don't."

"Who says I don't like him? I like him a lot. I got him the Zell, didn't I? And now I'm getting his poems turned into songs and out to a whole new audience."

"And you're screwing his wife."

"Stop it now. Even if I was," I say, "it wouldn't mean I didn't like Matt." The comment is so ridiculously revealing that both Gloria and I can't quite think of anything to say after that.

$\sim$

TONIGHT, WHEN MATT GETS home, Cara is sitting at the kitchen table playing cards with Eli and Lia. He greets his children, puts his phone down on the table, and has them listen to "In The Mooring." Cara sits expressionless while Eli and Lia cheer. They ask questions and say they can't believe how well the poem works as a song, the singing beautiful and way cool. He appreciates this. His children's support means a great deal. He glances toward his wife and gauges her reaction. For as long as he can remember, he's been attracted to her. Handsome and hale, a glorious Nordic girl, even late in the day she somehow avoids looking worn. Tonight, however, is different, the deepening of her eyes and firm pinch of her mouth anything but appealing. Her annoyance with him, her refusal to support what he is doing, cuts hard against his skin, slices deep to the bone.

Gloria's voice fills the room as Lia replays the song. Matt listens with his eyes closed now. Transported, moved by the music and how Gloria's phrasing stirs him in ways he had not been sure his heart was still capable of, he lets himself go. When the song ends he looks again at his wife, considers all the possibilities, here and there, inside and out, then shakes through the shoulders as if to toss off all extramural thoughts. To his surprise, the opposite occurs as everything else falls away and he is left to stand within the chorus of his poem, tethered to the construct of his own wane mooring.

Cara waits until the song ends before getting up, pushing against the table, and heaving a sigh as she says, "Well there, now you've done it."

And he in turn wonders, asks himself, *What have I done?*

~

We work the next six nights, record eleven tracks, and send them all to Glassnote including the five of Matt's songs. I phone Daniel and let him know he should check his email. We are late into August now and classes at the university are about to resume. The nights are warm and this evening I sit out back in the garden. It's the first night I haven't been at Colossal in almost a week.

Cara calls me daily now. We meet in the afternoon before I go to the studio. Each time I am with her I tell myself it will be the last. When she says she loves me, I ask her to stop, though I do so softly, in a whisper which suggests I am overwhelmed by her words. We have sex at the Red Inn off exit ninety-three where Cara seems excited by our marginal surroundings and throws herself onto the bed with purpose and vigor. Each day I have to hurry out afterward to get to Colossal on time, the scent of Cara's sex washed from me quickly with the coarse motel soap.

I sit sipping a beer on one of the garden benches near the Judas Tree, contemplating the advent of the moon, when Lidia appears in the yard. Fred greets her excitedly. I get up, happy to see her. We haven't spoken since our conversation at Caber Hills, though I have meant to call her. Lidia kisses my cheek. I'm glad she's accepted my invitation to check out the garden and I tell her so. We walk toward the fountain where a hidden twenty-gallon tank of water circulates through invisible tubing, releasing the water into a shell-like blue and beige pool. Lidia is wearing flip-flops, blue shorts, and a T-shirt with the face of Dave Archambault II embossed. She has brought me a beer and expresses how beautiful she finds everything, the fountain and the hill and path and flowers. "Who knew something like this could be made here?"

I let her take everything in before removing the cap from my beer and putting it in my pocket.

~

DANIEL GLASS CALLS ME the next morning. Fred and I have gone for a walk out toward the river, where we see wrens and crows flying together beneath the rising sun, and back. I have only just settled in to write and am trying to complete my draft, which is up to date now but without an end, and hearing my phone ring, I look to see that it's Glassnote.

Ten minutes later I am phoning Matt and Gloria. Daniel digs the songs we sent. He is definitely interested in signing Gloria and would like to discuss further. For now, he is thinking to remix three of the cuts and completely rerecord four more; he feels the remaining songs have come out great, including "In the Mooring" with which he'd like to test the waters and conduct a soft launch. "I want to shoot a video at Colossal," Dan says, and can I get that done for him? "Nothing fancy," he's thinking an in-studio look, with the camera focusing on Gloria performing in her element. By this time next week, assuming the contract is signed, Daniel wants to have Gloria up on Tidal, SoundCloud, YouTube, Dailymotion, Vimeo, ZippCast, Pandora, Apple Music, and Google.

I'm happy as hell and tell Daniel, "Yes, of course, I can handle the video." I call a filmmaker friend of mine, Veri Lane, and tell her what Glassnote has in mind. Veri's a fantastic artist, she is sure she can get us what we want and looks forward to meeting the band. I spend the rest of my morning trying to write. My protagonists are at a crossroads, their relationship near collapse; I have no idea what will happen next. Cara calls and I break our date, I say only that I have an early meeting that afternoon. Matt arrives at Colossal as I do. Gloria and Veri and the rest of the band come in soon after and we set up. Veri films us getting ready, films the band with Gloria as they play their way through a simulated version of "In the Mooring." We review the footage and do a few more isolated shots until Veri says she has what she needs. As the band is here, we decide to try recording one of the songs Daniel wants recut. I take Dan's notes, take my own new ideas, and guide the band through another pass at the song.

We work until around eight, then break for the night and have a drink. Frankie brings out the booze left over from other nights. We have half-full bottles of whiskey and gin, some wine recorked and good enough to finish. Gloria and Matt sit together on the couch. All three members of the band take shots before heading to late-night gigs of their own. After a toast with Wild Turkey, Frankie leaves as well. I sit across from Matt and Gloria and try as I have all week not to give off guilty vibes regarding my sleeping with Cara; I am watching Matt for signs that he may suspect I have.

For her part, Gloria is cordial with me and is more attentive toward Matt. Shoulder to shoulder, they joke and tease, aim barbs at one another, then laugh and joke some more. Matt is drinking steadily, mixing whatever is closest to his glass. I study his mood, the way his excitement for the songs appears to be cast over a gloom, his engaging with Gloria delivered with a dead-catch hitch in his eyes. We toast our music again. Matt sits with his right arm stretched over the back of the couch. Gloria shifts closer to his reach. I don't wish to make too much of their proximity; I tell myself artists are always interacting this way. We talk for a time about the Glassnote contract, making sure Matt's rights to the poems are ironed out with his publisher. After this, we circle back to discussing our music and the first song we rerecorded tonight, the poem "Heart Crush Spirit Flight," which is a work of intense exposure, a love story told from the perspective of a man attempting to rescue a wounded jay.

I love the music Gloria has written for the poem, the nimbleness of her guitar and voice as she conveys the damaged want of the defeated lover's effort. I've no intention of bringing Cara into the conversation, though the prescience of the poem is telling, the piece written over a year ago. I wonder what Matt was thinking at the time, but I am careful not to ask as we confer about the tune, only here Matt says suddenly, "Cara doesn't like the song. Any of them. She doesn't think much of them in general." He drinks his gin straight with melted ice, tips his head back, the stretch of his throat laid bare.

As the pretext of creating the songs was to impress Cara, I feel a need to say something, even though I don't want to. "I'm sorry to hear that." I say only this. We've not spoken of Cara in any real detail while recording, our concentration on the music, though I knew, of course, from what Cara told me, she was not pleased by my working with Matt.

"She thinks it's all a gimmick," Matt says. He has no idea why she's so hostile toward the songs. He uses this word "hostile," while Gloria rubs his shoulder, soothes him with whispers and pats his thigh. Her physical engagement seems entirely unnecessary, yet natural and not designed to make me jealous. I wish she would stop, I wish she were trying to get a rise out of me as this would mean she still cared, but her interaction with Matt comes across as instinctive and without me in mind. I reply to Matt and say that I'm confident Cara will come around.

"I don't know." He shakes his head too hard. "Things are different."

"An episode is all," I respond. "All relationships have their hiccups." I describe Cara's reaction to the tunes as just a blister burst, which will heal soon enough.

"Don't know," Matt says again. He drinks whiskey after the gin. I avoid making the same mistake and go for beer. Gloria offers her thoughts then, taking the conversation in a direction I don't expect, tells Matt to be mindful of Cara's mood. "A woman doesn't create static without a reason." She plays this card, presents herself as expert. I shoot her a look, I try and cut her off, but Gloria is determined to fuck with me now, at least that's what I think as she tells Matt, "If things in your relationship with Cara are changing, you need to accept that these are not arbitrary or indiscriminant alterations and should be treated as part of a natural progression. Change is organic," she says, clearly mocking me now.

"Jesus," I say and argue against the advice, insisting that rough passages are part of the process as well and that Matt is untested by this sort of matrimonial stress; his worry is mostly fear in the extreme. "Don't overthink anything right now," I say. "You and Cara will be fine."

Matt looks at me a half-tic too long, and I feel the heat beneath my collar begin to rise. "The truth is," he says, is that he's given the situation a good deal of thought. "Things do change," he tells us. "This is what I need to accept. I'm grateful for my marriage." He states this in the most departed way.

Gloria squeezes Matt's hand. Moved by his confiding, she takes his face in her own hands and kisses him on the top of his head. Matt blushes. I watch while he reaches back for Gloria, lets his fingers drift onto her shoulder where they remain. Annoyed now, I remind Matt that he was the one who spoke about the permanence of love and our need to hold tightly, but before I can get too far Matt drinks down the rest of his glass and excuses himself to use the bathroom. Alone with Gloria, I dive right in and bark, "What the fuck?"

Gloria laughs. I tell her I'm serious and she laughs again. I accuse her of purposely giving Matt bad advice, of flirting with him just to mess with me, that it's all a ruse and what she thinks I have coming, but she denies the charge, tells me to get over myself and repeats what she said the other day, "I like him."

"It's okay to like him, but you're messing with him now."

"Seriously? You're telling me this?"

"I'm just saying."

"What are you saying, McCanus?"

"You're the one who told me not to fuck with them."

"Yeah, and did you listen?"

"All the same," I say, "I don't think you should lead him on."

"Is that what I'm doing?"

"It looks to me."

"Stop looking, then," Gloria says. "No matter what we're doing, it's none of your business."

"But this is so wrong," I tell her. "For a hundred reasons it's wrong."

Gloria's drinking wine and is staying away from the liquor. Her head is clearer than mine, she remains composed, doesn't so much as change her tone as she says, "The only thing that's wrong is you thinking you have any sort of say. Matt can do what he wants and so can I. It has nothing to do with you and me. This is what you can't understand."

I ignore all this and more desperately implore Gloria to, "Stop, please."

She groans and answers, "There is nothing to stop. I'm not doing anything."

"You're not?"

"Nothing I wouldn't do with anyone I liked."

"Hell now. Hell," I toss up my hands and say, "This is Matt, for fuck's sake. You know where this started. You know where things are now. You know he loves his wife."

"Do I?"

"Yes."

"This from the man who's fucking her."

"Jesus," I say again and look back through the studio for Matt.

Gloria pushes the sleeves of her T-shirt up over her shoulders. Her arms are pure sex; every inch of her skin affects me this way now. She tells me I'm being ridiculous. "Matt and I aren't seeing one another, we're just collaborating."

"Very funny."

"Matt is one of the most rational and sweetest and most creative people I know." Gloria insists, "All Matt is doing is focusing on his needs." She says the problem with Cara is my fault, that I alone made things worse by sleeping with her. "Remember?"

"I remember everything," I reply and move to sit beside Gloria on the couch. I speak of how I remember her in my house, sitting in my chair, playing her guitar, sleeping with me, the warm smell of her, the way I miss her now and how this paper-thin construct we call love is harder for me to doubt these days, and how ironic is that? My knee is against Gloria's. I mean for my comment to convey a romantic optimism, a sense that none of us know what is in the stars and that there's always hope, only Gloria has tired of my persistence and says, "I'm not interested, Eric."

She kisses me unexpectedly, then moves away and says what's really sad is how I've learned nothing from my exploration of open relationships, and says, as Lidia before, that I am not open at all or I would understand things better now. She says my affair with Cara reveals a disturbance in my heart. "I sleep with who I like," she tells me, "while you fucked Cara for no good reason."

This invective is administered just as Matt is returning from the bathroom. Hearing his wife's name, he stops yet catches none of the content. Wobbly on his feet, clearly drunk, he has trouble coming as far as the couch. I get up, take hold of his arm, and suggest calling it a night and ask Matt for his keys.

"Whoa, partner." Gloria stands now, quickly and ready to challenge my claim, and grabs Matt's other arm, a wishbone effect as she tugs and whispers into his cheek, "Come on, lover, give me what you got and let me drive you home."

CHAPTER SIXTEEN

INSIDE THE CAR, MATT slides down in the seat, touches the tip of his nose as if completing a test, and asks, "How much did I drink?" I verify his mixing whiskey and gin, the eschewing of caution, and say with only a hint of lampoon, "Some combinations are more lethal than others."

Gloria is following behind in her car. I'm driving Matt's Jeep. I will drop Matt off at his house and then Gloria will drive me back to Colossal for my car. I have Matt with me only because I managed to snatch the keys first. I'm glad Matt is not with Gloria, but find being alone with him is awkward as he starts thanking me for everything I've done and then blurts out in a burst of glee, "I'm in love."

"Of course you are. With Cara."

"No. I mean yes. I mean no, with Gloria."

I dismiss the possibility and tell him, "You're drunk."

Matt rubs at his eyes and blinks. "Maybe," he says. "Don't tell Cara."

"That you're drunk? I think she's going to know."

"No, that I love Gloria."

"Stop now."

"You won't tell her, will you?"

"Why would I tell her?"

"Because you're friends."

"You and I are friends, Matt."

"Yeah, but you and Cara are *friendsier*."

I turn my head from the road to look at Matt, who is trying to push himself more upright on the seat. If he is insinuating anything I can't tell. I look back at the road just in time to catch a stop sign. Matt has his window down, his right arm stuck out for no apparent reason. I turn left, come up from the market, then east and into Matt's neighborhood where I try and get Matt talking of things other than Gloria and Cara. My effort is unsuccessful, however, so I turn on the radio and catch the end of Marian Hill singing "Back To Me." Matt listens for a minute then changes the station.

I find the house and pull into the drive. Gloria parks at the curb. I turn off the ignition and hand Matt the keys. "All right then, you good?" I'm looking to make a quick exit, get Matt moving toward his house so I can scoot to Gloria's car and speed away. Matt isn't quite done with me, though; he leans into the space between the two seats and asks plaintively, "What should I do, Eric?"

"Go inside," I answer, "have a shower, and get in bed with your wife."

"My wife doesn't want me."

"Bullshit. You're being dramatic," I say. "Quit feeling sorry for yourself. If you're going to fix things with Cara you need to man up."

Matt grunts as if my comment has inflicted an actual wound, and, realizing I may be coming at the situation all wrong, I attempt to correct myself, double back, decide perhaps being conciliatory will work better, and go ahead and let Matt know, "I get it. Gloria, right? She's something, and here you are all vulnerable and depressed by what's going on with you and Cara. It's been sudden and will likely blow over in a day or two, but for now you're missing your center and you feel you don't deserve this. For twenty years you've been devoted, and why should Cara be upset with you? It's unfair and here comes Gloria turning your poems into songs and she's beautiful and open and friendly."

"You make it sound cliché."

"Life is cliché, Matt."

"No." As drunk as he is, Matt maintains a poet's perspective and replies in turn, "Life may be a story retold a billion times, but that doesn't make it cliché." He says this just as the porch light comes on and Cara appears out front.

~

GLORIA SEES CARA AND gets out of her car. *Fuck.* Before I can do anything, Matt is exiting the Jeep while Gloria begins walking up the drive. "Hello?" Cara calls down. "Matt? Eric, is that you?"

What choice? I step into the driveway and say, "It's me."

Gloria walks directly toward Cara, hand out as she says, "Hello, I'm Gloria." Cara has her own hand above her eyes and is squinting through the dark and the glare of the porch light as Gloria approaches. Matt slides past the hood, following after Gloria, or going up to Cara, I can't be sure. He's not yet steady on his feet but better than before. When he gets to the steps, he grips the rail.

Cara says something to Matt, then turns and walks inside. Gloria and Matt follow. If I had a set of car keys I'd take off. As it is I'm tempted to hike home, the distance to my house only a few miles. The night is warm and I start down the drive, but here Cara comes outside again and calls my name.

I stop only after she threatens to follow after me. Already she is asking questions, motioning me toward her as I turn around. I answer that Matt had too much to drink after we finished our video and we were driving him home. "That's all," I say in reference to everything and nothing. Cara gives me a look that suggests she is about to harangue me again over working with Matt, then changes her mind. Despite her disapproval regarding my spending any time with Matt at all, she wants me near and invites me into the house.

I shouldn't, and there is no explaining, but in the light of the porch, with the stars above and the canopy of night framing her, in her T-shirt and no bra, her large breasts as I have touched and sucked and done more with than I care to mention, in shorts which show the smooth wonder of her thighs and bare feet made wide on the planks, I find myself aroused. Still I avoid Cara's hand while I climb the steps; I tell her to send Gloria out and we'll be off. "Don't be silly," she answers in a firm excited way and, taking my arm, ushers me inside.

~

MATT HAS PUT MUSIC on the stereo, Miles Davis's *Bitches Brew*. He has brought glasses to the table and ice, a bottle of gin and whiskey, and more wine. The front room with the stereo is all wood, the floor and shelves, the furniture and trim. There is a large red rug with a light blue and gold weave centering the floor. On the rug Gloria is swaying to the sound of Miles Davis' horn.

~

FROM THE DINING ROOM, through the open French doors, Matt can see Gloria moving to the music. If time and memory did not exist he could create from this vision a life they would have already had together. How perfect he imagines it would be. Of what came before, he doesn't want to think about now; he is determined to accept that things change and go the way they do. What lasts and lingers, lives and disappears, he can't explain—he can only address what is there now in the rhythm and release of song.

~

I SEE MATT STARING after Gloria, marveling at the possibilities, indulging in the fantasy, giving himself no caution when Cara comes back inside and says about the booze on the table, "Haven't you had enough?"

"Possibly," Matt replies. "I'm not sure."

~

I APPROACH GLORIA AND say in a half-whispered urgency, "Let's go." She smiles as if she hasn't heard me at all, she is dancing still, her hands in the air. Although her movements are light, there is resistance in her face as she twirls and looks at me and finally answers, "Let's not just yet."

Cara comes and stands beside me. Matt has filled his glass with either water or gin, I can't be sure, and entering the front room he does a sort of shimmy step that is supposed to mirror a dance. Gloria turns toward him and together they wiggle, while the music builds through the playing of John McLaughlin and Lenny White, Bennie Maupin and Dave Holland, Chick Corea on piano and Miles's horn like a sensual fog snaking its way around every note. I go back to the kitchen and then to the dining table where I pour whiskey over ice. One by one the others join me. Cara puts down coasters for our drinks, small square pads of mock-straw. I sit on the far side. Cara takes the chair next to me. Matt and Gloria sit across. The kids, Eli and Lia, are out for the night. Both of Matt's hands are wrapped around his glass. When he looks at Gloria, his fingers continue to dance.

"Do you want to hear something funny?" Matt puts the question to the group, though he is eyeing me. Cara taps my foot with hers beneath the table. I sip my whiskey as Matt says, "I saw you. A few weeks ago at the market. Cara and I were there. Do you remember, Cara? I said, 'There's Eric McCanus' and Cara said, 'Who?'" He appears amused before going on. "Three days later you showed up at SunGreen and then at our house."

"Imagine that," Gloria feigns surprise.

I downplay the coincidence while reminding Matt, "We shop at the same market. Our houses are close. The city's not that big."

"No, it's not," Matt says in turn. "I suppose we've been together at shops and movies and plays before, even readings and on campus dozens of times without knowing it."

"I'm sure that's true."

"Could be," Matt says. "Probably. But that was the first time I saw you. At the market."

"And three days later," Gloria can't resist.

"Eric came to see me," Cara says possessively, tying us this way, touching my arm up high beneath the sleeve.

"It makes me wonder about the way things happen," Matt again, turns toward Gloria, his head tipped so close I think he might put it all the way onto her shoulder. I nudge Cara to see if she objects, but she says nothing. "Anyway," Matt sits up, glances back in my direction. "I'm glad we met. I believe our meeting is a good thing."

Gloria leans closer to Matt's chair and says she's also glad. "Here's to building gardens." She raises her wine and Matt goes, "Hear, hear."

Cara is sharing wine with Gloria. I am looking still for a chance to make my exit, I am about to say, "On that note," but instead Matt continues to speak of coincidence and how, "I suppose it's never so much what brings people together but what we take from it at the time. I mean, every encounter is different, based on when we meet."

"Timing is everything," I attempt to be glib, hoping my condescension will get us to move on to something else, all this talk of the how and why and when people meet making me anxious, presenting a prelude for things I don't want to discuss.

"For example," Matt says, "if we had met five years ago, you most likely would not have read my poems. My first book was only just out, and what were the chances you were looking to have a garden made then?"

"But now," Gloria encourages Matt to go on. Cara reaches and pours more wine into her and Gloria's glasses.

"But now." Matt touches Gloria's wrist shyly, then moves his fingers away as if the surface of her skin is hot. "Now, when you have read my work and are looking for a garden, we meet."

"And even after the confusion with the Zell, we're here." Gloria references the Zell intentionally, as a way to remind Cara of the dispute between her and Matt.

Not that Cara needs prompting, her toes continuing to work against my calf, her chair too close to mine as she says of the Zell, "What a disaster that was, Matthew," and shakes her head.

"And yet," Matt has no more concern for what happened then, he is excited solely about now, how turning down the Zell led to my offering him a chance to work with Gloria. "And from there," he says as if the whole thing is a sweet little mystery, "what are the chances for any of this?"

"It's not about chance." I find myself arguing despite my desire to leave and say, "We're here because Cara's a landscape architect and you are a poet, because I run Colossal and Gloria's a musician, because I wanted a new garden, because I read your work and invited you to apply for a Zell. It's all threads in a weave."

"And not by chance," Gloria goads, then touches Matt's shoulder. All this unnecessary touching is beginning to piss me off and I hold up my hands to show that I am without occupation.

Matt says, "It's true, chance or not, from where things started it's hard to imagine we'd wind up here."

"But here we are." I try and narrow the scope of Matt's comment and say, "Our sitting together now is unexpected but easily explained. Nothing's arbitrary. Even the things that surprise us most are set in motion by something we've caused to happen."

"That's for sure," Gloria again.

"Right." I'm growing increasingly uncomfortable and try to clarify my original statement saying that the encounters we have are instigated by deliberate decisions. "I wanted a garden. I met Cara. Cara is married to you. We can trace exactly how things went step by step along the way."

"Oh, I'm sure we can." Gloria continues to fuck with me.

I shoot her a look, which asks her to cut me some slack, then say, "When I first met Cara I could not have known she was Matt's wife."

"Or that you'd become friends."

"Friends, yes. Me and Matt."

"And Cara."

"Right."

"You could not have known any of this." Gloria is enjoying herself.

I focus on Matt and say, "When we first met we couldn't have known we'd wind up in the studio putting five of your poems to music. But we can see how it happened."

I shake the ice in my glass, I do not want to go down this road at all and am hoping Gloria will let things end here, but she can't and says again, "Because of the Zell."

"The Zell," Cara repeats, sounding mordant.

Gloria is obviously pleased to see me struggling. My head is starting to ache as I reply, "Not just the Zell. The Zell was a mistake. Was my fault. I was hasty and didn't mean to cause trouble."

"It's not your fault," Cara wants to assure me.

I am starting to think if any of this is to be resolved I need to be more direct and say, "But it is my fault and now you two are bickering and that's no good. Your marriage is a significant achievement, while the Zell, the songs, and whatever else is irrelevant really and nothing for you to be fighting about. In the grand scheme nothing else matters but the two of you."

Cara is puzzled by my statement and asks what it is I'm saying, exactly. I want to quit talking and attempt to do so by groaning loudly and asking in turn, "How did we get onto this?"

"Matt was commenting about the coincidence of your meeting," Gloria remains amused as she offers her reply.

"Okay," I frown once more. "All I'm saying is, having gotten to know the two of you, I realize your marriage is what matters. What you have makes me jealous."

"Are you jealous, Eric?" Cara pounces on the word.

"Envious," I try this.

Matt addresses my choice of words as well, asks what I have to envy given how I don't believe in marriage. I answer, "It isn't that I don't believe. I can imagine many ways that marriage works. Yours works." I try again to reinforce; I am desperate to have Matt and Cara reconcile so I can bring a close to this craziness and get back to my life. "The fact that I personally have failed does not disprove love's existence."

"But we're not discussing love," Gloria corrects me. "We're discussing marriage."

At this everyone laughs. I am hoping that's the final salvo, but Gloria won't let go and questions me specifically as to my advocacy of open relationships and the supremacy of individual needs. I reply, "That was a long time ago."

"You don't feel that way now?"

"I feel individuality is essential to any relationship," I answer this way and admit in terms of open marriage and loving freely that I made a mess of this myself. "And to be honest," I find myself saying, I try to stop but it's too late as I stare at Gloria and confess, "I would give all that up, the open involvements and easy connections, to have one great love."

"Really?" Cara exhales.

"And yet at our dinner," Matt reminds me.

"At our dinner," Cara, too, is eager to hear what has caused my conversion.

I attempt to qualify my statement and say that I meant, for purposes of this conversation, I would exchange one great love for the rest, though Gloria remains relentless, a thorn, as she picks apart my words to argue, "You're assuming great love can't exist in an open relationship."

"I didn't say that."

"And what if there's no such thing as one great love? What if love's greatness isn't a constant?" Gloria continues to screw with me while Matt, too, is ready to jump in.

Emboldened, Matt surprises me by asking as follow-up to Gloria, "What if love is not eternal but rather finite? What if the love we have to share ebbs and flows over time, spreads like water so that what was once a great liquid pool winds off in other directions? What then?"

I am near panic now and stammer out some such thing about love as the only constant and how it's people who weave in and out, but this comes out all wrong and here Matt, in reply, leans into the table in such a way as I can already predict what's to come and as I need to stop, the thing he's been leading up to all along, heartened by poetry and booze and the heaviness in his heart caused by Cara's distance, the hollow ache he as a poet needs to fill, he can't hold back though I am desperate to stop him, I am about to reach for my whiskey and purposely spill the bottle, topple everything, make sure Matt doesn't go on, only I am too slow as always, a count behind the beat as Matt looks across at Cara and me and asks, "What if, for example, I'm in love with Gloria now?"

He says this so assuredly, so matter-of-factly, that we all freeze and then begin to laugh even harder than before. We are laughing still, the four of us, so hard that Cara has to catch her breath and all but shout over the rest of us to say that she and I are having an affair. Oh how we laugh at this, too. How funny it is, the suggestions from both of them, the things now said at last.

~

I AM THE FIRST to stop laughing.

Matt gulps at his drink, which I am sure now must be water. He waits until Cara is no longer laughing before asking the same as in the car, "So what happens next?"

I pretend I don't know what he means and ask for clarity, but Matt has turned from me and repeats his question to Cara. "What now?"

"Matt," Cara says his name softly.

For a moment we all wait. With just these few words Matt has directed us to where the evening feels destined to go. No longer as drunk, adrenaline administering to his sozzled state, he looks to me as if I alone have the answer. I don't, of course, but I get up from my chair just the same and go and kiss Gloria hard on the mouth.

In the moment I am perfectly clear as to why I do this, though even the explanation I give myself is crazy. I want to put an end to all, to make a statement and clarify where things actually stand, but my action is clumsy and what sort of reaction do I expect? Maybe I'm thinking Matt will stay in his chair, will gauge from my kissing Gloria the folly and futility of his own claim, will come to his senses then and return to Cara who I also hope sees me kissing Gloria as clarification and proof about us.

For her part, which is critical, Gloria lets me kiss her. It is only after we finish, after she has warmed to me and given me more than I expect, her mouth open and directing mine to where I almost lose my focus and forget where I am, only then does she release me, and, smiling in a way I wish she wouldn't, as I know exactly what she plans to do and show me, how if I love her it has to be this way and on her terms, she gets up and goes to Matt.

In his lap she sits and kisses him. Matt moves his arms, opening, receptive, taking all that is offered, and settles his arms on Gloria's back, allows himself to be kissed then kisses in turn, he shifts his hips so that Gloria can sink even further into him. They are as this, entwined and tender, together before us so that when I look away to find Cara, I expect she will be livid. Sure, yes, she is guilty of having slept with me, more than once, and mistakenly we both have professed our love in a babble corn sort of blurting out though neither one of us meant it. I assume this will be the reckoning, a healthy dose as Cara will howl and Matt will stop himself any second now, realizing there are lines drawn, which already he has crossed and should not go any further, while Cara will cry "Enough!" and dismiss all that has happened to date as a temporary madness.

Instead she comes and stands in front of me, begins to reach and draw me closer, is eager to kiss me, too, and what is this now? I have done as much before, sure; I have had sex in groups and gatherings, have played in places where managing my desire was not a concern, have had no misgivings and enjoyed myself even when the manifest in hindsight turned out to be something different than I thought going in. With Lidia I was arrogant, I could not handle what I believed, I lost my way and never really recovered. Here, though, I hope to benefit from my experience, I will call time-out and champion clearer heads, for Matt and Cara's sake, as they deserve to know what I have learned, that there is no taking back the things we do, and such decisions as pertain to the urges of the heart should be embraced with a certain caution.

Oh but I am a dog as Gloria knows. I am anything but cautious, I am without prudence the way a fish lacks lungs. Here is Cara in front of me, her curves and shape and skin so warm I can feel the heat. How hot is she, and don't I know? Our sex before has been entirely raw and unrefined, brutal and vanquishing, somatic as cell to cell we engaged and do so now as Cara leans in and I kiss her flush, my hands already sliding up beneath her shirt, her hands on my hips looking for their own point of engagement.

Gloria has moved from Matt, she has left his lap and brought him standing so they are embraced and kissing not three feet from Cara and me. What a puzzling mix we are, what a queer temptation and the manner in which I am expected to sort through it all. This is not free love for me, not in the sense that I have taken to it before, as I would prefer Gloria step away and be with me. I am not accepting and in no position to be offering, and yet the further we go the harder it is to remember all that, to focus on what may be of concern, until I can't help but give into the moment, the tug-pounce-howl, I am liberated against myself, I am taken in and gone.

CHAPTER SEVENTEEN

WHAT FOLLOWS IS JUST that.

I spend two days writing straight through at every hour. The story is nearly complete. It is different than what I saw coming and I want to get it down while it's still fresh.

Cara stops by late the next day and we talk. I do not know what to expect and am relieved to find she hasn't come for any reason other than to let me know she's okay. I give her the chance to say whatever needs to be said, I am understanding when she tells me it's too soon for her to know what last night means long term, though she does apologize for ever saying that she loved me. Somehow she thought the claim was necessary. I understand and joke, "Novice's mistake."

We sit in the front room, on opposite sides, Cara on the couch and me in the chair. She is dressed for work, in bibbed shorts and a T-shirt beneath. I want to ask about Matt but decide not to. Cara tells me just the same. I think to apologize as well, to say I'm sorry for everything, but the sentiment seems unfair now, the decisions made not mine to appropriate from Cara and Matt. I recall how in the middle of our sex last night, as Cara stood naked and stripped me down, as Matt and Gloria moved to the couch leaving Cara and me to fend for ourselves on the rug, as we entertained and took ourselves exactly as the evening offered, I marveled at the way Cara and Matt seemed to freely embrace the experience while I continued to suffer, the emancipated soul turned to flesh and soft tissue.

As we switched off then, husband with wife and old lovers together, the reality of what we were doing took yet another measured slice from my heart as I clung to Gloria in a way I had not before wanted Cara. The emotion seized at me, the degree of its intensity. I looked over at Cara and Matt and there again I was surprised as I found them entirely fine, fucking in the way the situation was meant, turned on by the bang-sweat stimulation of enabling one another to be first with someone else. This is the sensual ideal, the erotic lift which came from the adventure, and what was I to do then when my head would not clear and all I wanted was to run with Gloria out to her car, drive to my house, and not let her go again? What sort of confusion had this sick love caused me, and why could I no longer dispose of it?

~

GLORIA COMES OVER LATER that night. I am working still, adding Cara's visit to my book, writing of her and Matt as they were when

Gloria and I left, cuddling and cooing, and how curious it struck me, how it was them together and not us. Gloria knocks and Fred barks as I let her in. She has her blue duffel with her; she wants me to think she's coming back or why else bring the bag inside? "Why bring it in?" I ask after she tells me no, that she's going to New York, that Daniel called her directly and she is meeting with him tomorrow.

"Are you staying here now?" I ask again about the bag.

She answers, "Only tonight."

We go into the kitchen and search the fridge for beer. During our drive back to Colossal from Cara and Matt's, we didn't talk much about what just happened, giving ourselves time to sort things out. I tell Gloria that Cara came by and she's good. I don't ask Gloria if she's spoken with Matt, though I do say that I've been thinking maybe I will take a moratorium on partying for a while, that I've had enough of the drama and would prefer to concentrate on us. Gloria does not so much address my statement as she says, "Matt's coming to New York with me." She tells me Dan wants to meet him, that "In The Mooring" is tracking well and Dan would like to discuss a deal where Glassnote invests in republishing Matt's poems.

I lie and say that I am glad for everyone. It appears my intent to forgo any further flings and only be with Gloria has run into a conflict. I ask Gloria if this is where she is now with Matt and all the rest, and she looks at me in that way she has which breaks me every time and she knows it as she says, "When wasn't I where I am now?"

We open our beers and stand at the counter as Gloria leans against the stove. I'm not sure that I can do this and tell her, "I don't know."

"Yes, you do."

"That was different," I mean about how I was before. "With you I'm just not into it. I don't want to share you."

Gloria corrects, "You're not sharing me, McCanus. It's not up to you."

"But that's just it. It's not up to me. It's how I feel. If it were up to me I'd chop silly mischief sticks and pass them out to you ten times a day, but it isn't where my head is now and I no longer want this. There's no epiphany here. I'm not a convert to the staid and traditional, this isn't a moral pronouncement, but rather I no longer get a rise having the woman I love be with someone else. I don't find the experience liberating with you. Maybe it's an age thing," I say. "Maybe I have reached a point where things slow down. This wouldn't invalidate what I'm saying. We all live in stages and episodes and this is mine now, where I am and completely valid. Only a fool fails to embrace what is right for them and what is right for me here is different than before, and this is because of you, because of my wanting to be with you, not yesterday or last year, but today. This is what I want and what is good for me."

I ramble like this without a breath while Gloria sips beer. She has on a sort of sun dress, a light mix of lime greens, sleeveless, which is belted in the middle by a thick sash. She doesn't seem pleased or annoyed with what I've said, she does not react in any visible way and is quiet for a moment before saying, as she has before only with a different sort of finality here, "You're so full of shit, McCanus."

Am I? I don't know. I say again, "Let's have a baby." This is the way things are done now, I say. I will put a picket fence around the front yard, will paint the planks white, will tend to all, mother and hearth, will conform my happiness to where it wants me now, and how content we will be. I tell Gloria that I love her and here at last she answers the same, and then after a moment she laughs, harder than last night when our guffaws were nervously extorted but more honestly. I join her, the liars that we are, we laugh until I say again I love you and this time I am all too serious and Gloria knows. She puts her beer down on the stove, walks back into the front room, collects her blue bag, and heads out the door.

~

IN BED, I THINK he must be, too, how he will listen for her, listen as I do now; listening for what isn't there. How softly she breathes. It's late and they have again talked well past the hour when the moon is full overhead and all the sounds outside have gone silent. He is thinking in the lateness that everything is fine, thinks, too, that everything is too much for him despite all they have said to one another, the promises and solidarity, the willingness to be together wherever that takes them as the journey is what matters and how excited they are by all now. Renewed, he knows that everything has changed and remains a wonder.

In the morning, he runs at the high school, pictures himself later that day meeting Gloria at the airport and flying together to New York. He will sleep with her if she lets him, he is sure he will though he already knows this time will be different. He wishes he were more like McCanus, free of concern and open to the moment. As soon as he thinks this, though, he understands it's not true. He rolls toward her, tries to embrace, wants her to embrace him as well, but she groans in her sleep. *Not her fault*, he thinks and rolls back over.

He comes home from his run and showers. The house is empty. He packs his bag for New York and heads downstairs. In motion, he doesn't want to stop, but on his way to the door he turns back. There is this then in the things that change. Ten minutes later, he's put two more bags in the trunk of his car and is driving east to the airport.

~

MY LOVER IS AMUSED when I tell her what has happened. It's like her to find the humor in stories such as this. We are again at our motel, at what she calls our motel though it isn't ours, wasn't ours before, and won't be ours after. I do not tell her so, I do not say anything after I finish with my story and have no answer when she asks, "So what happens next?"

During my silence she watches me the way I imagine a Zander fish tracks a worm. When she starts to laugh and throws back her hair, I don't know whether to feel relieved or angry. I settle on the former as she starts to undress me.

We are as always for the moment, warm on the blanket, warm in the sheets, warm in the warm spooned cradle. I lie again in the days that come, lie as does she. Prone, yes, I am prone here, prone in every way. I turn flatbacked and reach for her to cling. "*Manuke*," she calls me playfully and brushes me off.

~

LIDIA COMES BY AND we sit on the deck and share a drink. I have started to dismantle the garden. After everything, I find it's not for me. Over the next few days I remove the gazebo and fountain and do away with the steps so that the hill I've created has to be climbed and descended on the slant. I cover the path and return to the lawn, I remove the extra flowerbeds but leave the trees, which are doing well and look almost natural in their setting.

Lidia is good company and we do not talk of why I leveled the garden. We do not talk of love or longing or any of the things that get in the way of enjoying one another's company. We avoid topics of real significance, though there is significance in sharing simple moments like this.

I have told her the story of Matt and Cara, much of it if not all, not the parts I don't yet know how to tell, but about Cara designing the garden and Matt turning down the Zell, how they wound up being a much different couple from when we met, and how was I to know? "These things," I say, "are hard to predict."

After a time, after Lidia has come back again and we are used to one another sitting together in what was the garden, with Fred running and digging through the remains, I do talk to Lidia about her baby. I feel this much is important and needs to be said. "About that," I start, and she pretends not to know what I'm referring to, she pretends in this way in order to get me to say it all myself, and so I do. I say to her then for purposes of clarity, in order to be as honest as I can, "I am happy for you, but I do wish it could have been us." I see as I say this that Lidia is okay with hearing as much now, and, feeling there's more to explain, I talk on, rambling as I do when I'm agitated or nervous. I say that I know it's greedy of me to want anything from her at this late date, but I do wish in hindsight I'd had a better sense of what we were doing, that I might have realized then how freedom was hard, and I do hope she knows I loved her, do love her, in my own way, which was never enough but remains all that I have.

"Anyway," I give a shrug. I can only be earnest for so long before the sentiment begins to bind too tight, and to this I chuckle a bit, the sound a silly bird's cackle as Fred runs between the trees and barks at the branches while I say to Lidia, as Gloria said earlier, "At least all of this has given me something to write about." I tell Lidia then about the progress I've made on my new book, so many years into the drafting, and how I think possibly I have a handle on the story, at least in part, though I confess I still can't be sure how the thing is to end.

Lidia in the sunlight, in the glow of all that comes at this time of day, how well she knows me and I appreciate that differently than before when love confused everything, when want and urgency and ambition were mixed and set to boil in the kettle, how Lidia knows and wants for me, wishes for me to be free and happy and nothing more, that there is no more, she knows, and says of my book, of the story I am writing and can't seem to finish because of all the confusion that remains, the wonder I have for what's to come and what to do next, she says of it all, of the pace and pulse and push I am still unsure how to handle, she smiles and touches my hand and tells me, "Then you'll just have to stop."

ACKNOWLEDGMENTS

MUCH THANKS AND APPRECIATION to the inimitable Tyson Cornell and his staff at Rare Bird. Julia, Gregory, Jake, Hailie, and Alice are the sort of folks who make publishing a smooth sail. As always, to my family, Mary and Anna and Zach, without whom nothing is possible. To all others, friends and partners in crime and business, thanks for the continued patience and tolerance with me while I pursue the madness that is my life as an author in search of something meaningful to say. Appreciate everyone and to everyone—onward.